# PENDULUM

*Books by A. E. van Vogt
available from New English Library*

# PENDULUM

## A. E. van Vogt

NEW ENGLISH LIBRARY

First published in the USA in 1978 by Daw Books

Copyright © 1978 by A. E. van Vogt

First NEL Paperback Edition July 1982

NEL Books are published by
New English Library,
Mill Road, Dunton Green,
Sevenoaks, Kent, a division of Hodder and Stoughton Ltd.

Typeset by Avocet Marketing Services.
Printed in Great Britain by ©ollins, Glasgow

Van Vogt, A. E.

Pendulum.
I. Title
813′.54[F]   PR9199.3.V38

ISBN 0–450–05477–2

# CONTENTS

# PENDULUM

'ALL RIGHT, Hud, that's it. Stop!'

Hudman had long ago formed the habit of translating all the English spoken at him into Frisian, silently, of course, under his breath, and then answering silently in Frisian and finally translating the Frisian aloud into English. As a consequence of this procedure, he was known as 'that slow Dutchman!'

He did the translation automatically as he stopped. Or rather, as he pressed the correct button on the controls there on the deck of the gently tossing vessel – those controls which telegraphed the stop message 2½ miles down to the massive equipment they had been setting up on the sea bottom for a week. The Frisian words that he undertoned were, '*Gooet, Hud, dat iss it. Stoppya!*'

He grew aware of a tingling in the fingers that touched the button, started to pull away, then let his hand freeze as another set of words boomed in his mind: '*Booska, Hud, manu fa coor. Yat!*'

'Glub!' said a startled Hudman aloud, in English.

Afterwards, he would remember that moment and what followed, and would realize what a fantastic and incredible event it was.

There they were, a hundred men on a ship in a calm, tropical sea. As far as vision could range was a seemingly endless, restless, glittering ocean, reflecting the brilliance of an early afternoon sun.

It was stiflingly hot; yet there was a relieving wetness – not humidity, but a spray – that came up to cool them whenever a large wave slapped hard against their low-lying vessel.

They were remote from the great world of humankind, doing their strange work in water over two miles deep, and suddenly –

He must have made an unusual movement, in some way reacted violently, for his companion on deck said, 'Hey, Hud, what'sa matter?'

Hudman remained where he was, vaguely conscious that he was not well, but making no decisions at all. There was an enormous confusion in his brain; pictures, sounds, voices, people, tumbling past his awareness in bits and pieces and flashes. An eye, a finger, a word, a window, a white cloth, a pair of blue pants, a woman's blonde hair done up in a bun exactly on top of the center of her head, a city in the distance, the glint of a stream – these were among the images that stayed with him long enough to be recognizable. The impression was that thousands, if not millions, of such flitted by his mind's eye.

Through and beyond that interior madness, Hudman was aware of the chunky Italian climbing off the observer's chair, and striding over to where he sat at the controls of the winch, swaying. And where, abruptly, without having any personal control, he started to fall.

'Hey, watch it!' said Sputoni in an alarmed voice.

As the man grabbed him roughly and held him, his leather jacket pressed against the reeling Hudman's cheek. And one of the things that was good about that was that the jacket was wet and cool from sea spray. And another thing that was good was that the arms were strong.

What the man's voice said was only partly good. 'How ya comin'? How ya comin'? Just tell me when you're okay, and I'll let go. Hey, you gotta heart attack or sumpin'?'

The final question penetrated what seemed like billions of mental images and voices, and brought a spasm of fear. 'Good Lord!' he thought, and for the first time in years he did not translate from the Frisian. 'Good God, is it possible? Is this what a heart attack is like?'

He was dimly conscious, then, of being half carried and half dragged over to where the helicopter rested in its holding chains and launch gear. And now one of the men had come out and down from the bridge and was helping to hold him. And somebody else's voice was yelling in the strange echoing way that voices sounded from a distance in sea air, saying, 'We'd better fly him to the island and get him medical help.'

For a long time after that, he lay on the floor of the helicopter with a pillow under his head. Sputoni sat in a seat beside him, and in his ears was the roar of the driving engines and of the rotor. And in his mind, the realization that he was beginning to feel better. The inner voices seemed to be receding into a remoter background, still there but no longer dominating.

11

With that increasing separation from the source of confusion, gradually *he* was again. A kind of normalcy returned then. And stayed.

Once more, he was in a mental condition of being able to decide things for himself, though there seemed to be nothing to decide.

Since he had had that particular obsession from his earliest teens, he thought about it. Soberly. Somehow, it had never previously occurred to him that in a personal physical crisis, a human being really had no choice ... *In what happened back there on the ship, I didn't have a single say. It was all automatic.*

Because he hated automaticity, he tried now, as he lay there, to think of a purpose he might have. After many minutes, all he had come up with was Wait! Wait and find out what was wrong.

He waited.

They had been operating for a month in the vicinity (within 500 miles) of Tengu Island, so they had their own landing location at the airport of the principal city, Askara. Nothing fancy. Just a flat, roped-off area and a shred marked *U.S. Government – Authorized Personnel Only.*

The helicopter squatted down in its noisy, but gentle, fashion. Whereupon, Sputoni went over to the adjoining shed and commandeered a jeep. They were presently driving along the main street of Askara to the office of the officially designated M.D., a Dr. Kyet.

Hudman, at first, sat stolidly beside the Italian. But presently his brows knitted. He wiggled in his seat. He looked around and up and away, showing awareness of his surroundings.

All by itself, that street scene was worth a couple, or three, or four, blinking glances. It was quite narrow, as if its builders had begrudged space for people.

There seemed to be room only for the shops, and for a two-way highway which the prospective customers, if any, shared with the automobile traffic.

Some very special customer types were on that street. After his first look, Hudman wet his lips, puzzled. After his fourth look made its visual survey, he sat up bolt straight. He said, 'Hey, Spute, look at all those guys and women in the blue pants and that funny white shirt.'

'Yeah,' nodded Sputoni, 'I been noticin' 'em. Must be a visiting warship in the harbor.'

Hudman said, 'Oh!' Then he said, 'Oh, of course.' Naturally, he thought, who else? He did notice that the way you could tell the girls from the boys was that they had blonde hair done up in a bun on the top of the center of the head. And that was somehow familiar, as if he had seen it before.

The explanation was good enough. And so for the first time since his heart attack – as he now accepted it to have been – he translated again into Frisian. The internal return of normalcy was that complete.

Sputoni accompanied him into the waiting room of the doctor's office. But he didn't sit down. Instead, he stood, looking ill at ease, shifting from foot to foot and parting his lips as if he intended to say something, and then didn't say it. Hudman grinned knowingly up at the chunky little guy, and said finally, 'Hey, Spute, while I'm here in good hands, why don't you slip over to Little Italy, have a snort, and talk Italian to the barkeep?'

'Yeah – hey, you gotta good thought.' The thick face looked sheepish, but relieved. Sputoni headed for the door.

Hudman called after him, 'Be back in, say, an hour.'

'Yeah, sure –'

Dr. Kyet turned out to be a handsome, brown-skinned, native islander. He spoke accentless American. After having his brown-skinned nurse make the stereotyped tests, he came in with a little chart in his hand and said, 'If that was a heart attack, there's no sign of it here. So it wasn't. You've got as good a ticker as I've seen in the last year.'

'*Dat iss gooet. Doe bist bedaanked!*' said an almost overwhelmed Hudman under his breath. And, a moment later, translated aloud, 'That's great. Thanks.'

It was still 20 minutes before Sputoni was due back. Hudman, bouncy now, decided not to wait. Moments later, smiling, relieved, ebullient, he stepped outside briskly – squarely, so to speak, into the center of a group of the blue-trousered men he had noticed on the way over.

Hudman apologized. 'Excuse me, gentlemen, I shouldn't have barged out like –'

He stopped. They were looking at him. All of them. At *him*. And they all had purple eyes – bright, large, slightly protruding – and whitish-gray faces. Also (it hit him instantly) there was a peculiar smell.

Hudman didn't actually connect the smell right away with the people. After all, this was exotic Askara. And just in the flicking of his gaze, there, not too far away, was an overturned garbage can, its gooey contents spilled on the combination sidewalk-road. Swarms of insects attested to the special over-ripe attractiveness of the yellowish puddle it made. Also, beyond that, a dog was in the act of defecating. And, beyond *that*, standing beside an electric-light post, one of the blue-trousered types was relieving himself.

That was about as far as Hudman's perception had time to take him into colorful Askara's main street.

The very next instant one of the blue-trousered men near him stepped closer, reached forward with a tiny, gleaming, pencillike object, and touched his hand.

... He was walking with the group. Not thinking about it. Not asking himself the sequence of logic that made what he was doing seem like an act of free will.

He still noticed things. Noticed, for example, how odd, really, was the white shirt that these people wore ... For Pete's sake, he thought, it's a big, wide scarf folded in the middle, with a frilled hole at the fold for the neck. The two bottom ends were, respectively, tucked into the front and the back of the blue pants. In between, on either side, whitish-gray skin was visible.

He was led by the young men into a cocktail lounge. Hudman noticed over the entrance the sign: HAGLE-STEIN'S BAR – *Stop and Wet Your Whistle, Friend*. And still he had no resisting thought. Moments later, he was guided to a corner table where a large man in the same type of dress – blue pants and white shawl shirt – sat watching his approach with a pair of large, purple eyes.

The youths paused at the table, and so did Hudman. Since it was the corner, he half turned, and so he saw his captors (which is how he thought of them later) each make a gesture with his hand. Sort of turning the palm smartly. A salute? Hudman wondered.

The big man responded in kind. Then, looking at Hudman, spoke slowly in English: 'S-s-i-i-t-t!' He pointed at the empty space across the table.

The gesture, and the word, in a vague way implied a command. And that triggered in Hudman first, a pause, and then a remote wonder about what he was doing here, for Pete's sake! The seated older man seemed to realize the problem for, after a hesitation of

15

his own, he said, 'Uh, pul-l-l-ee-ee-se.'

It was visibly the right approach to the deep, timeless source of resistance inside Hudman. Without another thought, he sat down in the indicated chair. Simultaneously, the man's hand gestured at the youths, and they departed.

Absently, Hudman noticed that they paused just outside the door, and waited there. For some reason, that seemed perfectly satisfactory, so he faced forward as the big man said, 'I'm having time –,' he paused and cocked his head as if listening, then '– hard time with English. But I have an interest question. What you doing out there on the water? I . . . not seem to get clear picture from your head. What you put down in the deep sea that stir my tomb?'

Hudman started to echo 'Tomb?' Abruptly, he realized that the other man had a problem with the English language, so he said, tentatively, 'The water is 2½ miles deep.'

'Hmmm.' The purple eyes were thoughtful. 'The earth crust really been pushed there. I wonder how long it take?'

'We're in the tropics,' Hudman explained in a baffled voice. 'That means the water on the surface is warm, and the water on the bottom, except for currents here and there, lies cold and unmoving. It's like a desert. No movement. No life. Forever.'

The man nodded, and spoke another of his enigmatic sentences: 'I sense we there, not forever, but very long time.'

'The surface of the tropical sea is hot,' Hudman continued doggedly, 'so we put in piping and set up a pumping system for bringing the hot surface water down there. Once that process starts – and we had just started it – convection begins. The warmed water roils upward, stirring bottom nutrients. Life stirs.'

'We stirred,' the man agreed.

'You're not the kind of life I mean,' Hudman said in a severe tone. 'The sea life cycle, where there was none before, starts. Tiny sea life, which brings larger life to eat it, which brings large fish. And where there's food, breeding can start, and go on as long as the roiling continues. We're putting down a pump system every 50 miles.' He finished, 'In a few years, fishing fleets will find in those waters enough edible fish to feed a few billion more people.'

'Good!' nodded the heavyset man. 'There lot of us. We need all food we can get.' He paused, frowning. 'The big problem ...' he seemed to be thinking out loud, for his eyes pointed off to one side, 'where we put everybody?'

In Hudman, at that point, came the Big Pause. Even a child can only listen to a limited number of sentences spoken at cross purposes, and he was a man who had noticed each apparently meaningless statement uttered by the other man.

It was full stop. And at least half a dozen double takes. A feeling of – for Pete's sake! Then, from pursed lips, tentatively, 'How many of you are there?'

Unexpectedly, tears welled into the purple eyes. 'It seem wrong,' the older man sobbed. 'Thirty billion people, and not even you have power to bring more than fraction here.'

'How do you mean, me?' Again, the feeling of being at cross purposes.

The tears were still spurting. 'Doubt we can rescue more than eight,' wept the man. 'As catalyst, you pretty good, but you only one person.'

'Eight billion?' said Hudman, faintly.

A measurable number of seconds passed by, at least 11 or 12. Across the table, the tears stopped spilling. Hudman involuntarily braced himself for what was, after another long moment, not clear. He was beginning to feel blank again.

Here was madness, and he was the mild-mannered type who did not attack aberration in others by direct confrontation. Unless, of course, it was aimed at him.

The chunky man was recovering rapidly. A smile suddenly brightened the gray-skinned face. 'My friend,' said this changed being, 'I want thank you for rescue us. We been wait a long time. My name Lluuan.'

Hudman went through his Frisian ritual, ending with, 'Thanks for what, for Pete's sake!'

'Who is Pete?' asked Lluuan, sounding genuinely puzzled. Having spoken, he made a decisive gesture with his left shoulder, pushing it forward. Simultaneously, he straightened in his chair. He said, 'First things have to be first. Listening you talk that funny language, and try to talk it myself make realize what we do first. We shall provide Earth with more basic tongue again. In accidental rescuing me, when you lower heating unit, you be glad know you have made possible transformation back to sane universal language.'

He broke off. 'I gather you always sense that problem yourself. Since you translate English into more understand language. Once you learn the perfect language, you won't have to go through that labor anymore.'

Hudman heard all the words, and even translated a few of them into Frisian. But it was a moment of shock, on another level. He had accidentally caught a glimpse of his watch.

'Good God!' he blurted. 'I've got to get back to my ship.'

As he stood up, there was in him still no sense of being a prisoner, or of having been one. The first tiny doubt came as he glanced at Lluuan's face. He had been turning away; now he paused, held by the unhappy expression in the great purple eyes.

Lluuan said, 'I have just sent out takeover order.' His mouth twisted uneasily. 'I been hesitate. Something in your mind I not quite get.'

'Take over what?' asked Hudman, frowning.

'The world.' Lluuan waved vaguely. 'In few minutes my men will have seize the stores, the police station, radio station, docks, airport ...'

Pause. The strange eyes clouded. 'Where those planes come from? And the ships?'

In the moment, at that precise instant, Lluuan gained a hearer who heard. 'Just a minute,' said Hudman, 'are you telling me that when the first hot water hit bottom – that minute when I had my false heart attack – we touched something down there $2\frac{1}{2}$ miles. And that released you and your – these?' Hudman gestured toward the youths who were waiting outside the bar and, faltering now, finished – 'from some incredibly long sleep?'

'Considering amount of water at that point,' nodded the big man, '"incredible" right word. Depth suggest hundreds of thousand years.'

'And you're going to take over the world?'

'We will do great good for everybody,' said Lluuan. 'Expect great progress.'

Hudman scarcely heard the promise. His attention had leaped to another, more practical thought. 'How many soldiers you got?' he asked.

Momentarily, the meaning seemed to slip by Lluuan. 'Enough,' he said. Came a hesitation. The face showed irritation. He gestured helplessly. 'Really,' he said, 'the English language.' He explained, 'We don't call them soldiers. They're – well –' He waggled a hand helplessly 'English!' He shook his head. 'Gulits, helpers of the –' He finished, 'It's actually untranslatable.'

He nodded rapidly, with abrupt determination, half to himself, half at the recalcitrant universe. 'Tomorrow morning in all schools we start teaching sane language.'

Silently, automatically, Hudman translated the exasperated comment into Frisian.

His internal communication was interrupted: 'Your ship, your work,' said Lluuan, 'is it, uh, not safe?'

The purpose of the question was not clear but there seemed to be a threat in it. As if Lluuan were trying to decide ... *decide* ... (a profound feeling of shock) ... *whether or not he'll let me go.*

The shock grew enormous ... *I'm a prisoner. That guy touched my hand with that – what? – and I walked along with those guys as if I was hypnotized.*

It was the instant reaction moment. The total resistance to the idea of anyone even for a minute telling him where he could go or, in this instance, where he couldn't ... time.

Hudman bent forward and reached across. Simultaneously, the six-foot-four Frisian frame of his stiffened, and that was all he needed to brace himself for what happened next.

The big man came up in his grip lightly, almost airily, as if he were made of balloon material. The stocky body brushed things off the table as Hudman dragged it across the surface and brought the thick face within inches of his own.

'Listen!' he snarled at the other's teeth and nose, 'I don't know what you're up to, but don't mix me in your affairs!'

The purple eyes, so close, stared into his calmly. Lluuan said, 'You must not scare of us. You are catalyst. We need you. I only try find from you what is best place for you right now. Later, you get special treatment. So, you tell me, where should you be?'

It took awhile, but in the end it was the older man's total lack of fear that soothed the savage feeling that had flared so swiftly and forcefully. Hudman continued to scowl, but he maneuvered Lluuan so that he could stand on his feet, and he was very gentle about it, merely making sure that the other would be able to balance himself. And thereupon released him.

Lluuan walked around the table, settled into his chair and looked up with a faint smile. He said, 'You very strong man, but not dangerous.'

Hudman blinked, and did not quite know how to react to the evaluation.

'Way you grab me,' the other man continued, 'strength in it, but no violence, no intent to harm. A defensive attack. Interesting, right? So, now, perhaps, you answer my question.'

Hudman said simply, ' "Catalyst" is a very significant word. So I'll make it straight. What happens if someone takes a pot shot at me and doesn't miss?'

Lluuan spread his hands helplessly. 'We disappear back to where we came from.'

'All of you?' Almost blankly.

'Every single eight billion,' nodded the chunky head, glumly.

'Good God!'

'Picture not completely clear,' Lluuan went on, uneasily. 'Maybe we find us all suddenly back in the tomb, waiting again. Maybe back in the sinking land, the last nightmare of tearing-apart continent. Not definite which.'

It took a few moments. Then, 'I've been at sea since I was 16,' said Hudman. 'Now, I'm 28.' He elaborated

21

anxiously, 'It's a big converted freighter. We been doing this job for nearly two years.'

'Oh!' Some of the unhappiness was fading from the heavy face. 'When you dock next?'

'We're due in here next week.'

'Our problem,' said Lluuan frankly, 'how to protect yet not make you mad. So –,' he nodded, half to himself, 'maybe back on your ship is safest place. We got big things to do. Get used to what world like now. Take care of trouble. When you dock, come and see me.'

Hudman didn't pause to argue. Out the door, past the little group of the blue-pants youths, off down the street to the Little Italy bar. Swift relief. Sputoni was still there.

'Hey!' he said, 'you got me worried. What the doc say?'

It was dark when they came down from a cloudless sky onto the brilliantly lit deck of the super-freighter that was their home.

Hudman chose to eat a fish dinner.

Afterwards, he chose to play cards.

Got sleepy, and decided not to argue with that.

As he headed for bed, from the room behind the bar where the card tables were, Sputoni called to him from a bar stool, 'Hey, Hud, tell these guys about those sailors we see.'

It took several moments for Hudman to translate that through his Frisian circuitry on to the realization that the 'sailors' referred to were Lluuan's people.

Sputoni was continuing, 'Ole Grue here,' he indicated the mildly grizzled chief electrician on the adjoining stool, 'say he never hear of any country with sailors dressed like that. But they're for real, right?'

Hudman, who had spent the late afternoon and

evening trying to make unreal Lluuan's evaluation of him as being 'not dangerous' – it meant that any decisions he made didn't mean anything – kept on walking. But just before he left the room, he flung a single harshly spoken word over his shoulder. 'Yeah,' he spat.

In the morning, the captain said over the intercom, 'We won't be putting into Tengu next week. Something odd going on over there – a rebellion, or something.'

The sea has a language, too – burble, splash, murmur, slap, gargle, hiss, whisper – the same sounds endlessly, is the impression. And yet, Hudman had discovered in his years of listening that the language of the ocean, though primitive, never quite repeated; yet, paradoxically, told a few simple stories over and over. But it was more like the story in music. It stirred the emotions and the senses, and did not have to be translated into Frisian.

The days went by. He sat at his controls on the deck. He listened to the language of the water. He helped put down one huge heating unit, then another, and others. The routine had a rhythm that was not unpleasant. Gradually, because the sea is remote and unconnected, the meaning and implication of what Lluuan had said began to waver in his head somewhere between reality and fantasy. Only the vaguest sense of threat remained on the eighth day when, about midmorning, the captain's voice on the intercom commanded the crew to come to the recreation room. When Hudman joined the men already there, he saw that they were gathered in front of the TV, and that what they were all staring at was a blue and white river scene, rather pretty and wild, with rippling blue waters and white foamy waves.

The river was being photographed from a helicopter, and it extended to a remote horizon; not just as far as the eye could see, but as far as the telephoto lens of a TV camera could focus.

Hudman stared, brows knit, frowning. Simultaneously, he tried to fit together two thoughts. The first was the action of the captain in calling him and the others from their work to come and watch television.

The second was that the river, while interesting in its odd, moving aliveness, was not exactly something the crew should be viewing during daytime work hours.

At that point, as Hudman had that critical thought, from the press of men behind him the voice of Sputoni projected a querulous question, 'Hey, where all those people comin' from?'

*People!*

Hudman had been standing up. Now, he pushed toward a chair and sat down. Abruptly.

Hudman watched the screen with narrowed eyes, appalled. He was remembering what Lluuan had said: eight billion. E-i-g-h-t b-i-l-l-i-o-n! The figure, the total of them was a threat of mindless proportions to a world that was half-starved with a population of four billion.

On the screen, the view had shifted down to the ground. The camera there appeared to be on a mobile unit, which matched speed exactly with the white-scarfed, blue-pants people, who were at this remote edge of that mass of walkers. Two reporters on foot approached a young woman, whose hair was done up in the familiar bun, and the young man directly behind her. They held up their mikes and attempted to interview, first, the woman, then, the man.

The two did not look at their interrogators, did not talk back, did not turn, or slow, or speed up, but simply walked on like automatons. Those, like Hudman, watching the screen, grew aware that a second man, who walked several layers deep inside that fantastic mass of people, was taking note of the reporters. In fact, in approximately a minute he had pushed his way over to them, and began to speak in the same hesitant English that Hudman remembered from his conversation with Lluuan.

It was this second man, now, who made a series of sensational statements, heard and translated all over the world.

He said, 'I am helper. We are from long ago, how long not certain, but long. I have permission from our Lluuan,' he used it like a title, 'to give information. In our two groups there are eight billion and several million of us. Our rescue made possible when connecting unit activate by heating box put in ocean by John Hudman. We very advanced scientific and mental civilization. Will help present day to new height. But we immediate need lot of food, which we will quickly increase by our methods. We request quick action from all governments. All available supplies sent quickly to Monterey Peninsula, west coast United States, and to north Holland, Europe. Our people will be out there soon help speed up shipments. We come in friendship. Nobody will hurt nobody. Everybody will benefit, first, by learning basic new universal language. Final comment, Lluuan want ship with John Hudman come quick to San Francisco. John Hudman, if you listening, it time for you talk to Lluuan again, for everybody benefit ...'

On board the good ship *U.S.S. Menasco*, all the everybodies of one accord turned and stared at Hudman. It was a total surprise for him, also. He sat there and the sweat poured down from his forehead.

An ultimate fear had come; inside him everything let go.

After awhile, after those numerous pairs of eyes had seemingly been accusing him forever, he said hoarsely, 'Look, I was up there on deck doing my job. Up there with Sputoni, he doing his job, me doing mine. All I did was my job. Just like the rest of you.'

In answer to puzzled questions from puzzled people, Hudman added defensively, 'Yeah, I had a conversation with this guy in the bar. He talked nutty, so I just kidded him along like I believed what he was saying was real. For Pete's sake, who'd have thought that a guy in a bar really meant it when he said that would happen.'

As he uttered the word 'that', he waggled one arm-hand toward the television screen.

At that point, Captain Eli Bjornson, a large redhaired Norwegian, walked forward and took charge. He cleared the big room. At that point, the captain was paged by the radio operator. He went off, and then his voice came on the intercom and instructed Hudman to come to the captain's cabin.

Hudman came in to find the commander sitting with phone in hand. As Hudman entered, the redhaired one held the instrument out to him, saying, 'The Pentagon wants to talk to you.'

Somewhere inside Hudman, good sense once more began to shut off. 'Slow Dutchmen' don't have too much going for them under normal circumstances in an exchange that requires thinking. In a crisis, they tend to go automatic. Early conditioning takes over. For long, far too long, long after they should keep their mouths shut, they're still innocently, naively, honestly giving forth with the facts. One of Hudman's conditionings was that your government is fundamentally your friend. And, since he was an employee of

26

the Navy, and knew the penalties for perjury, he accepted the right of the military to any truth that he had.

There was, even in him, a sense of relief, the feeling that now, thank God, he would be under the protection of the authorities.

After a while, the voice on the phone said, 'Put Captain Bjornson back on!'

Hudman handed the instrument over dutifully and, also at Bjornson's request, left the cabin and returned to his task on the main deck. It was there that he finally, a little late indeed, shut his mouth.

A sound!

Hudman blinked and opened his eyes on pitch darkness. It took a moment then, to realize – somebody knocked.

Even as the belated awareness trickled through his sleep-ridden brain, knuckles rapped again on the door of his cabin.

Sleepy blinking, sleepy thoughts, and then, 'Hey!' he called, 'who's there?'

'It's me, Les Reed, radio operator.'

'Oh, yeah, Les.' In the darkness, Hudman sat up and groped for the switch on the bed light. 'What's up, Les?'

'Got a message for you, from General Laroux.'

The light was on now. Hudman was aware of his crumpled pajamas, bare feet on the cold floor, a sweaty sleep smell, and of the clock embedded in his night table. It showed 2:24 A.M.

He also had a rueful realization. His long-time dislike of the ship's radio chief was now proved to be one of those stupid judgments that people rendered upon their fellow men without evidence. 'Slimy son of a gun!,' he had once labeled Reed. True, the words were spoken after one drink too many, but they were,

27

in fact, a vociferation of his until-then secret opinion.

Damn nice of the guy to personally bring him a message at this hour of the night.

'Yeah, just a minute, Les. I'll be right there, Les.'

One, two, three, four steps. Doorknob cool on palm. Unclick lock with little finger. Turn knob. Move awkwardly out of the way of the door as he swung it open.

The six foot mustached type, who stood in the hallway, had his right hand behind his back.

'Hi, Les, what's the message from this – I never did quite get the name straight when I was talking to him – General La – La –'

'Laroux,' said Les Reed. He moved his right hand from behind his back and there was a gun in it. At that final moment, he must have been moved by an unslimy qualm because he muttered, 'Sorry, Hud, General's orders.'

The next split-instant there was a bright flash and the roar of a pistol, echoing and reverberating in the confined distances of a long corridor.

In Hudman's brain, a million, billion, jillion images skittered. Oddly, they were like what had happened the first day, when a kind of energy had backed up the winch from two and a half miles down in the ocean. Once more, there were the faces, the strange buildings, cities seen from afar, glowing sunsets, trees, plains, rocky beaches, and people, people, people, all with purple eyes and wearing blue trousers and white shawl shirts.

At the very tail of that visual spectacular, Lluuan's face came out of the confusion and floated into sharp focus. The purple eyes stared at him calmly. And the remembered voice said, 'Thou art safe, Hud. The Gulits, who to thee reach through my connection with thy mind, offer thee total protection. But we do have a severe problem with this general. When we took over the Pentagon late this past evening, he was gone.'

The voice continued, 'The method used to save thee, an imbalance created in time. The imbalance will, for awhile, continue. Like a pool of water that has had a rock dropped into it. It moves in waves and ripples. In thy circumstances, may on remote shores briefly lap. –'

As he came to the branching corridor with the other arriving seamen and passengers from several ships, Hudman hesitated. His feeling was that he was on the right when he should be on the left.

On the surface, no thought touched his brain. While he paused, the other people moved past him and off to the right. Whereupon, he turned and strode by himself along the leftward passage. As he started to pass three young men in blue pants and white scarf-shirts, one reached out and touched him. '*Doe comt dissa vie,*' the youth said in halting Frisian. *Lluuan fwar de vaaghtya.*' (Thou come this way. Lluuan for thee waits.)

Hudman seemed to find that instantly satisfactory. Yet, he spoke his original intention, '*Ik praekesaer Ik vol an kaemer seekya, dan vol Ik Lluuan comma varr.*' (I considered I will a room look for, then will I Lluuan come to.)

The youth said firmly, '*Lluuan fwar de vaaghtya, meen hair.*' (Lluuan for thee waits, my lord.)

Hud was driven in a jeep by a blue-trousered, shawl-shirted, gray-complexioned man along familiar streets that swarmed with other blue-trousered people. The streets also swarmed with San Franciscans. And that, of course, meant that here were the inhabitants of one of the three American cities – the other two being New York and New Orleans – with that special character that comes from too many old, dirty buildings and too many people with open minds.

At the fourth stoplight, Hudman, who had been born in the Bay city, could restrain himself no longer. With a single twisting movement, he vaulted off the jeep, calling over his shoulder, 'I'll be right back.'

Moments later, he was confronting a typical San Franciscan, a well-dressed Japanese gentleman.

'I beg your pardon,' said Hudman.

As the other paused uncertainly, Hudman explained quickly about having just arrived on a ship, and of having heard of the takeover by way of radio and TV. 'What is it like?' he asked. 'What's happening? How is it affecting you?'

'Too many people,' was the polite reply, 'and not enough food. But one good thing. Fifty or so people who move into my house, all learning old Japanese dialect I spoke in my childhood. Very interesting. I learn their language. They learn mine. Excuse me.' He stepped past Hudman, and walked on.

A girl, who had a very light version of dark skin, was passing. Hudman fell in step beside her, made his explanation, and asked the same question. She gestured vaguely. 'There're thirty of these people living in the same room with me,' she said in a distracted tone. 'We sleep in relays. But they're very courteous. Two girls share my bed, and the others sleep on the floor, and they're all learning Tagalog, a language I spoke as a child in the Philippines. Goodbye.' She broke into a run, and quickly disappeared around a corner.

A hand grabbed Hudman's shoulder from behind. 'White boy,' gritted a voice in his ear, 'what you do to make that little dark girl run like she's scared?'

Hudman sighed inwardly, and simultaneously twisted and reached. On such matters he was never slow, and so, in a flash of powerful movement, he found himself face to face and eye to eye with interlocked arms and hands, with a six-foot-four black.

'Hey!' said this individual, 'you're kind of strong, huh. You must be one of those tough guys like the kind that raped my great-great-grandmother.'

Hudman sighed again. This was an aspect of glamorous San Francisco that the invaders had apparently not yet dealt with, so it was up to him. 'How do you know your great-great grandmother was raped?' he asked wearily.

'Look at me close,' said the man. 'See all the white blood in my face. Those cheapskate lips and small nose, and the whitey shape of the head.'

'Look,' said Hudman, flatly, 'my great-great grandfather didn't do it. Because I'm a Russian sailor, just arrived in port. Right now, what I'm interested in is all these strange types in blue pants. I keep hearing stories that this is an invasion. How's it affecting you?'

The black's face, so close to his, abruptly acquired a disgusted expression. 'I run into more Russians –' he said gloomily. 'Last three white girls I tried to mug, and make 'em pay for my great-great grandmom's bad experience, were all Russians, expecting to be let off the hook because the great Soviet Socialist Republic secret police would come around here looking for me if I so much as harmed one hair on their heads.'

He broke off. 'Those blue pants arrive in black town, and I hit the streets.' He showed his teeth and grinned. 'Okay, sailor, you got one thing goin' for you that's better'n bein' Russian. You're as big as me.'

He started to shove Hudman, and had one fist drawn back for what was evidently intended to be a farewell attempt at removing a tooth or two, or perhaps even an eye.

31

At that exact instant ...

... Hudman was sitting in an office facing Lluuan. This time, what separated them was not a barroom table but a gleaming executive desk, and they both sat comfortably in large leather chairs, with a huge window behind the chunky man. The scene visible out there was of San Francisco Bay.

So the waves haven't lapped too far, he thought.

More important, he had already got information that was not available on the *U.S.S. Menasco*.

Sitting there, gazing at the gray face and strange purple eyes, Hudman began to feel better. Not just a little better, a lot. He could feel the change inside him. Even as he noticed that inner stimulation, the sense of well-being jumped to a higher level.

He realized what part of the feeling was. He actually was being protected on a fantastically high level of superscience.

Even more significant, the implication was that he was a key figure, indeed. These people did need him, exactly as Lluuan had stated that first day on far Tengu.

With that feeling and that thought brightening him, Hudman indicated the view and said cheerfully, 'Pretty, eh?'

He was slightly surprised, then, to observe, for the first time, that his host was not cheerful at all. Lluuan was staring at him gloomily. The heavyset man said glumly, 'Nobody could get message into your head. All time you talk to the Pentagon man, different Gulits use my mental connection to you and take turns to say, 'Hud, please shut up!' 'Hud, don't say anything!' 'Hud, keep secret what spoken between Lluuan and you!"'

It was not the moment for Hudman to explain about the psychology of a 'slow Dutchman,' even if he had known what that psychology was – which he didn't.

Lluuan was continuing. 'Hud, what we going to do with that mad general up there in orbit?' He gestured vaguely at the ceiling.

Hudman thought *Laroux is the general who tried to have me executed –*

*Tried!?!* Pause. Then *was that all that happened?*

An ever so faint doubt stirred deep in his mind. It was so faint that he, so to speak, brushed aside the momentary anxiety that came. But the underlying thought diverted his attention.

He felt his brows automatically knit into a frown. 'Lluuan,' he said, 'I don't understand what your Gulits are doing. Suddenly, I'm in San Francisco. Suddenly, I'm sitting here. No transition. Tell me quick what it means before it happens again.'

As he finished speaking, he realized something. His need to know was suddenly so intense that he had forgotten to do his Frisian thing. His words and thought were English all the way.

The chunky man gestured dismissingly. Yet, when he spoke, he seemed to answer the question. 'Many trained minds work together, can twist time,' he said. 'But process not easy to stop. Like a pendulum has lot of motion. Take a while to come to full stop.'

Hudman mentally digested that for a few seconds. Finally, uneasily, he said, 'First time it happened, it lasted – my guess – less than thirty minutes. This time, I've been sitting here maybe five minutes. Do you think we'll be able to be here thirty minutes, also?'

He saw that Lluuan was nodding. 'Each time a little longer, with exceptions. We must try not to have one of the exceptions. So, better not right now have anything happen that put you back on that ship. Avoid going back to where it start. That could slow things. On ship, maybe months before next time. And finally end up with twists last fifty years instead of fifty minutes. Way to avoid, not think about. Change subject, yes.'

Somewhere in there Hudman noticed he was no longer feeling quite so great.

After a long moment of blankness, he was able to have a different thought. So different, in fact, and yet apropos, he felt himself grinning.

He said, 'I have a message for you from Sputoni. He wants you to leave the Italian language alone. Particularly, don't bother an Italian settlement in southern Switzerland where they speak an Italian variation of Rhaeto-Romanic, which Spute claims is very close to ancient Latin. It is called Für Lan.'

On the other side of the gleaming desk, Lluuan looked pained. Then he closed his eyes resignedly. 'Just a minute, Hud,' he said. Silence, then, 'I getting a telepathic connect-up through a Gulit in Für Lan country.' His eyes remained closed. He seemed to be listening intently. His lips parted. He spoke slowly, as if he were repeating words he was hearing, and then translating aloud.

' *"Che devio far?"* (What should I do?) *"Uto famio plazhay?"* (Can you do me a favor?) *"Doliy izza chesso?"* (Where is the washrom?)'

Lluuan shook his head and opened his eyes. He said, 'Pretty language. But like most tongues on earth today, not so good as Uxtagooganazan.'

Across the desk from Hudman the white shawl-shirt wiggled as the older man shrugged. 'No problem,' he said. 'We solving language problem. In each situation, we learn their language, they learn ours. Soon, everywhere people speak sane language. Only one problem. Somebody must touch Laroux, so we have control him.'

34

Hudman's mind went back to what the Philippine girl and the Japanese man had told him in his brief street interview. He nodded. 'When I get back to the ship,' he said, 'I'll tell Spute that you're being very skillful about the way you're teaching your language, and –'

His voice came to a faltering stop. *Did it!* He thought. *Just like that came back to talking about the ship. Next thing you know I'll start wondering what actually happened when Les fired his gun –*

And that automatic reaction came to a mental equivalent of a skittering halt as Lluuan said shakily, 'Hud, don't think thoughts like that. My Gulits all holding positive feeling for you. The healing process needs lots of positive –'

Time twisted.

... Captain Eli Bjornson awoke to the sound of scratching on wood. He opened his eyes ... Pitch dark.

The strange sound continued; seemed to be coming from the corridor door. Frowning, the officer turned on his bedside light, slid the automatic pistol from under his pillow, released the safety catch and lurched off the bed. Only seconds later, he had the outer door open and was staring down at the man who sprawled there with one outstretched hand still fumbling at where the door panel had been.

'*Hud!*

It took awhile. Because he had to drag the long body over to his office couch. And with much gasping, had to lift it onto the couch. As the ship's official medical technician, he recognized shock when he saw it. And, since any severe condition had to have a cause, he undressed the man and examined the body.

He made a puzzling discovery. There was a lot of

half-dried blood on the skin. But the two wounds, one in the stomach and one in the back where the bullet had evidently emerged, were both essentially healed.

Bjornson wiped away the blood, cleaned the wound areas, and injected a suitable chemical for extreme shock. Then he pulled up a chair and sat through the wee hours waiting and listening to the mumbling voice on the bed.

Only three times did the commander lean forward and probe for additional information. The first time, he said, 'What did you do to Les Reed?'

It developed presently that Hudman had stepped forward, grabbed the gun, and smashed the radio man over the head with it.

When that information was finally clarified, Captain Bjornson hastily picked up his phone and called the night duty officer. (It later developed that Reed had a concussion, but would survive. But it would take awhile.)

The second time Bjornson evoked a clarification from Hudman, the latter muttered, 'I'm getting mental messages from Lluuan. He wants me to talk to the General.'

'Well,' said the commander, 'are you willing?'

That was the third probe; and the answer was, after much mumbling, in the affirmative.

'Well!' repeated the red-headed man in his heartiest voice, and added, 'First, you'll have to get back on your feet. And then, when it's physically feasible, we'll have to be careful that the SOB doesn't get another chance to put a bullet into you ...'

The rendezvous, when it finally took place, was on a mountain top in Baja California. The advanced type shuttle lift settled straight down, almost like a shooting star except that its computerized landing mechanism, in the final few hundred feet, slowed the vehicle to a touch stop as it hit the ground. A few minutes later, a helicopter settled nearby. After some cross-signalling, Sputoni and the general climbed out of their respective carriers at about the same moment. The latter patiently submitted to being searched, then allowed his shuttle to be entered by two engineers, who next came forward from the helicopter.

Laroux was vaguely amused. 'These poor nuts!' he thought. 'They don't realize that all this means nothing. My position is absolutely impregnable, my power likewise absolute.'

Fifteen minutes went by, and then a second helicopter zoomed over a nearby height and landed on a rocky ledge a hundred feet away. Out of this emerged Hudman. As Hudman walked toward Laroux, Sputoni backed off and eventually took up a position on a height about fifty feet away. He produced a pistol, and waited with it casually in one hand.

All around was nature in the raw, and in front of Hudman stood a slender man in a smart uniform. Face to face, to Hudman's considerable relief, the shining individual turned out to have the voice that he had heard a month before on the radio-telephone. The officer looked tense, forty, and was awesomely loaded with gold braid and decorations. Slightly overwhelming was the effect, but Hudman braced himself and said, 'Lluuan wants to know what you want, sir.'

Human behavior has a language of its own. Like any other language, it 'just growed,' acquiring its rationality, if any, late, late, late in its development.

That language was as articulate inside General Laroux as it was in Hudman. He was a trained man. And so, when Hudman had originally described the little device with which the purple-eyed man had touched his hand – and instantly hypnotized him – he recognized superior science and anticipated total takeover. Within ten minutes, personnel at Cape Kennedy began maneuvering great rockets into firing position. One by one, the beautiful monsters took off for distant orbits.

So did Laroux – take off. By the time he, also, was safe in an orbit, the whisper of human nature was providing a steady flow of communication inside his skin, down in his groin, and particularly in that special part of the brain which ceaselessly perceives and feeds back unmonitored automaticities.

As a consequence, a basic thought passed up into the conscious level.

It murmured, 'I have tried to do my duty. My first act, in attempting to have this man, Hudman, assassinated, failed through no fault of mine. My second action, in orbiting nuclear weaponry, has a terrible drawback in that, whenever a bomb is dropped on ten million invaders, it will simultaneously kill a million Americans. So, I'm actually in a bargaining position. To begin with, why don't I, first of all, use that atomic threat to right an ancient wrong?'

Two men standing on a mountain top deciding the fate of the world.

A wind was blowing. It blew from behind Laroux and ruffled his hair. It blew into Hudman's face, as cool as a sea breeze in the tropics. It made faint, wind-blowing sounds. And yet Hudman's impression was of intense silence.

Abruptly, an improbable thing happened. In front of him the lean, stern face of General Laroux relaxed into a grin.

The officer said, 'I shall be glad to tell Lluuan, through you, exactly what we want.'

The grin faded. The voice went on, 'Hud, I want you to recall Shakespeare's line, "There is a tide in the affairs of men which when taken at the full flood –"'

The grin was back. 'Hud, we are the two lucky people in all this. Everything we stand for can now come true.'

Once again, the smile disappeared. Or rather, took on a distinct satiric twist. 'You and I make a team, my friend, such as never before existed. You with your telepathic rapport to Lluuan, and me with all that power up there in the sky.'

'Uh!' agreed Hudman, numbly.

'Before leaving Washington,' said the general, his voice brisk and bright, 'I got your dossier from the Navy. I noticed that your father was Frisian, and your mother three-quarters Russian and one-quarter Nez Perce Indian.'

'Hey!' said Hudman.

He was amazed. He hadn't thought of his mother's family since the death of his father in his teens.

Hudman drew a large breath. 'General, what are you leading up to?'

The shining creature in front of him seemed to freeze. Then, 'I've been in touch,' he said simply, 'with the Provencal Separatist Movement.'

Pause. Hudman stared blankly because, amazingly, the older was gulping as if his own words had triggered profound personal emotion.

Abruptly, fantastically, tears splurted. 'When I was a child,' sobbed General Laroux, 'I spoke Provencal –' He looked mistily at Hudman, explaining, 'It's the original French language,' he said.

'Oh,' nodded Hudman, 'a provincial French dialect.'

The face in front of Hudman seemed to be considering the comment. Finally, 'It's the real French language,' said the general.

'Oh!' said Hudman.

The officer's face now had a petulant expression, but his eyes stared to one side, as if he were contemplating an inner unpleasantness. Suddenly, his teeth showed. 'Those damned Parisian French!' he snarled. 'Imagine, the language of the great troubadours of the Middle Ages, the language of the greatest lyric poetry ever written, ignored and degraded by those stupid pragmatists in Paris.'

Hudman, who knew nothing about the past history of other European dialects, other than Frisian, had been watching the awful performance uneasily. His own awful feeling was *I'm really looking at myself* –

First, Lluuan, automatically accepting that the language he had learned as a child would make sense in the hearing centers and voice boxes of two hundred million Americans accustomed to speaking the peculiar Low German version of a Low Dutch dialect called English. Now, here, Laroux, with Provencal, a dialect of an outrageous language – French – in which virtually not one word was pronounced according to the natural sound of the letters by which they were spelled.

'For Pete's sake, General –' he began.

As he reached that point, he saw that the officer was visibly trying to recover. The man swallowed several times. Then he took out a handkerchief and wiped his eyes.

Hudman did a little swallowing himself, and then he said with determination, 'General, what you and I have in common is something called race consciousness –'

The instant that he spoke the fateful words, he had a distinct awareness of the meaning echoing down and down inside him. A startled realization came.

This was the first time he had *ever* allowed the analysis to surface. Always, in the past, there had been the feeling that if he ever did examine his motives, the underlying 'reality' would be threatened.

He saw that General Laroux seemed to have recovered from his own repercussions. The man stood now, staring at him. Or rather, studying him thoughtfully.

Hudman forced himself to continue. 'This whole matter of obsession with one's language of origin has been a big thing the last few decades with millions of people. But each person is obsessed with his own dialect, and not with yours or mine. And so –' Hudman drew a deep breath – 'here you are with Provencal . . .'

'And,' the lean face was smiling, 'here you are with Nez Perce.'

Hudman, who had his mouth open, intending to speak further, kept it open for many seconds. Only when spit began to drool out and over his lips did he close them and simultaneously reach for his hand-kerchief.

General Laroux continued with the same, faint, knowing smile. 'It's been my experience, Hud, that Americans with Indian blood tend to get interested in their Indian background.' He urged, 'You did learn Nez Perce, didn't you?'

Hudman was wiping the drool off his chin. Twice, then, he started to deny the words, and each time couldn't speak. *Couldn't admit* that it was Frisian he had learned. A memory came of himself at his father's funeral at age 16½. That was when he had made the Big Decision: 'My dear, wonderful dad, so long as I live you will never really be dead. I promise with all my heart to keep alive forever everything that you stood for.'

At sixteen, one tended to get things mixed up. His father had never, in truth, stood for Frisia and Frisian. He was the third generation, product of that period when the melting pot still made sense, when children were still ashamed of their parents' foreign accents, and when English seemed to be one of the logical international languages to be learned as a matter of simple good sense.

'I –' began Hudman, vaguely.

He literally couldn't go on. The thought: Somehow, General Laroux' wrong deduction protected his father's sacred memory, and simultaneously protected his own interest in the Frisian language from ridicule and from whatever might go askew in this whole Uxtagooganazan madness.

With that thought, that need to defend, he was finally able to speak, and even to be devious, for defensive reasons, of course, in what he spoke about.

Hudman said slowly, almost thinking out loud, 'Yeah, I was interested once in Nez Perce. But you can't really make a large certainty out of being one-eighth of anything.' The words, the thought, spoken aloud, triggered a memory from long ago. 'Hey, you know something, General?'

The man did not reply; merely stared at him, waited.

Hudman continued, 'There's a story that comes down that Indian family side. When the white man first came to Oregon, my great, great, etc., grandfather, you know what he said?'

The gray eyes fixed on his blue, and waited again.

'"There's got to be an end to them somewhere. There can't be many more, surely." General,' Hudman spread his hands, 'so far as the Indians were concerned, we whites came out of nowhere, just like these Uxtagooganazans.'

The expression on General Laroux' face indicated that the comparison left him somewhat less than enthralled. 'The early American settlers,' he said, 'were individualists. These Uxta– Uxta–' He paused, looked disgusted, then continued firmly, 'Uxtans seem to be a singularly regimented race –'

'Who knows,' interjected Hudman, 'what the early settlers looked like to the Indians.'

'And, furthermore,' continued Laroux, as if he had not heard, 'they don't hesitate to use their hypnotic gadgetry to regiment everyone they contact. So –'

Abruptly, he did an amazing thing. There he was, standing beside a tall shrub. The ground under him, under them both, was broken rock, and they were high enough so that the view in every direction on that clear, sunny day was sensational – that is, if you liked to see miles and miles of mountain desert from a height. There he was in that remote wilderness, and suddenly he straightened, stood at attention, and spoke in the formal tone of a general addressing an officer-aide.

He said, 'Mr. Hudman, tell King Lluuan that unless he does what I want I shall have those bombs up there –' he did not point, but he looked up ever so slightly – 'drop one by one on large concentrations of Uxtans.

'What I want,' Laroux continued, 'and hear this carefully! In France – the whole of France – the language to be taught in all the schools for all future time will be Provencal, and –' the formality seemed to sag a little and he smiled a tight smile, 'here in the United States, the national language will be Nez Perce – forever.'

'Uh!' said an astounded Hudman.

As he stood there, almost blank, Lluuan's voice spoke inside his head. 'I have, with my Gulits, in those places where live these people, checked quickly. The

43

Provencal language has many non-French words in it, but enough French-type to make it easy to teach like he want. Nez Perce, name given Indians in Oregon by French, means pierced noses. Language very pure, but simple. Has much meaning about hunting and fishing and animals and wilderness. Not technical. So, easy to teach. Make no real difference anymore. Everybody, by our mind-to-mind method, now speak sane language. So we just add Nez Perce in United States, and Provencal in France. We keep skillful suggest everybody their own language fade. So that soon happen.'

Through the entire mental message, Hudman had his mouth open to explain that his interest was Frisian. Yet, by the time Lluuan was finished, the feeling of resistance had faded. He felt resigned ... *Did it again*, he thought, hopelessly.

The real thought was that the nuclear bombs up there were too deadly for him to start arguing against the certainties of General Laroux.

It took a little while, then. General Laroux insisted on back and forth conversation. Clarifications. 'Let me make completely clear,' he said, 'that in every other part of the world they can teach Uxtan. It's probably a good thing for there to be a universal language to replace peculiar sounding tongues like Japanese, Chinese, Russian, Hindi – you know, all that junk out there.' He waved an arm, taking in half the horizon.

Hudman was bracing himself, thinking, 'Somewhere in here I'm going to have to have a talk with Lluuan about leaving the Frisian language alone –'

An odd tension accompanied that half-decision. It occurred to him that the feeling might portend the next Time Twist.

But the seconds went by, and there he still was, so he began to back off. At twenty feet, he yelled goodbye. At forty, he shouted 'yes' when Laroux called out that the two of them would get together again at a future time.

Presently, safe inside #2, Hudman watched the mountain top recede and the great mass of land below take on the essentially featureless appearance which characterized the surface of the earth when seen from a great height.

Down on the ground, the process of the original arrival continued its reverse motion. The two engineers emerged from the shuttle and hurried to helicopter #1. Sputoni, thereupon, scrambled down from his high perch, trotted past Laroux, and also climbed aboard #1; at which point, Laroux somewhat hastily reentered the shuttle.

There was, now, a slight variance from the straight reversal condition. The shuttle, which had originally arrived first, was faster and more powerful than the helicopter. It took off abruptly and climbed at a speed that quickly left the whirly-bird behind. The appearance was of an awkward crow competing with a hawk or a falcon.

Within the hour, the *U.S.S. Menasco* was taking evasive action. It headed rapidly due south, trying to look like just one more large coastal freighter. That was while there was still daylight. As soon as darkness fell, the big ship swerved west.

A disconsolate Hudman sat in his cabin and watched the dark ocean through his porthole. He was gloomily realizing, once more, that what Lluuan had said about the Time Twist thing slowing down if he ever got back on the ship (the starting point) was all too true. He recalled unhappily that Lluuan had even mentioned a time length like fifty years. (But that, as he remembered it, was for a later swing of the pendulum.)

Boy, he thought, what a life I've got ahead of me!

And, worst of all, it was all automatic. Not a single decision, not one moment of choice, nothing for him to make up his own mind about.

The almost-blankness of that realization was still going on when his intercom buzzed. The voice of Captain Bjornson said, 'Hud, would you like to come to my cabin for a chat?'

Hudman knew only too well that he was listening to a command. But the wording fitted perfectly with that poor, defeated part of him that kept saying he had a right to make his own decisions.

'Yeah, Captain!' he decided out loud, gratefully. 'Yeah.'

He put on his shoes, walked along the lengthy corridor, up one flight on the elevator, and knocked on the door with the brass metal letters on it spelling the word PRIVATE.

The commander's muffled voice sounded from beyond the panel, 'Come in, Hud.'

Hudman did so. But after he had shoved the door shut behind him, he stood just inside, uncertain. The cabin's interior was more dimly lighted than he had ever seen it before. The single lamp on the desk was on. Captain Bjornson sat at the desk, and he now indicated the chair at the side of that desk. When Hudman had shuffled forward and seated himself, Bjornson said, 'I been thinking about this whole business, Hud.'

He stood up, reached over to the locker behind and to one side of Hudman, took out two glasses and a half-full bottle of liquor, poured the glasses full to the brim, set one in front of Hudman and the other on the desk next to his own chair into which he now settled himself again. 'Let's talk about it, Hud. What we going to do?'

As Hudman took his first sip, the redheaded man,

seeming to forget his own liquor, leaned forward earnestly and said, 'My family comes from a part of Norway where they speak a local Norwegian dialect known as Streele. I suppose that's all going to disappear now.'

Hudman, who was suddenly feeling quite sleepy, nonetheless thought, 'For Pete's sake, another dialect!'

Aloud, he said, 'Is this, uh, Streele just a local accent, like the southern way of speaking English in the United States, or is it a real regional dialect?'

'Genuine dialect,' was the reply. 'Regular Norwegians can't make out the meaning at all.'

'There must be a billion different words on this planet,' mumbled Hudman, 'all sacred. Even Reed,' he continued, 'turns out was willing to put that bullet in me because his family comes from a part of England where they speak a different accent, which he imitates once in awhile as if he's joking. But he really isn't.'

'Yep.' The answer sounded far away, and the person who spoke it was vaguely visible to Hudman through a blur of sleep. 'So the question becomes, can we really let all this happen?'

'I don't know how you're going to stop it,' Hudman replied, 'unless you put another bullet in me, and Lluuan and his Gulits can't protect me a second time. I have the feeling they're trying to reach me right now, but I'm too far gone in sleep.'

The equally far-gone voice, that came from the direction of the redhead, said, 'How about poison in your liquor? Can they protect you from that?'

'I was just gonna say,' said Hudman dully, 'that's a pretty strong drink you gave me. 'I –' He stopped, slumped far down in his chair, stared through a dense fog. 'Huh!' he said.

'And if that doesn't work,' said Bjornson, 'maybe we can chop you up into little bits and pieces.'

'You so-and-so!' said Hudman, as he slipped off the chair onto the floor.

'Sorry, Hud.'

Hudman lay for a while, eyes closed, only partly awake but thinking that he was on the floor in Captain Bjornson's cabin.

Suddenly, a different awareness ... Ground! I'm lying on grass, for Pete's sake!

He blinked. Then he flicked his eyes open. Then he sat up.

He was on a hillside. In the distance below him, a city stretched to every horizon. There was crystalline glitter in that city's buildings, and a golden sheen, and silver reflections from a million gleaming points, with great slashes and flashes of purple and red. It was a city different from any Hudman had seen in his numerous voyages.

Exultant realization came. 'Hey!' He spoke the words aloud in English (Frisian suddenly seemed very far away and unimportant) 'Another time twist!'

Enthralled, he scrambled to his feet. And he had his first glorious thought of where this swing of the time pendulum had taken him. The golden, silver, crystal city – somehow he knew it was so – was in ancient, vast Uxtagooganaza. Before the disaster, before it sank into the colossal depths of what, at some future time, would be the Pacific Ocean.

Up there in the 20th century, he was presumably dead – poisoned or cut up. But good old Lluuan and his Gulits had managed to balance themselves in that time period by precipitating him millions of years back.

How long would it be this time? The worry about that was a remote emotion, as distant as the Frisian inside him had suddenly become.

As he started down the hill, he was like the emigrant to a new country – eager, excited, determined to fit in, with no thought at all about his past, no sense of race consciousness, ready for the melting pot.

It was the great moment of dedicating himself to this new world.

# THE MALE CONDITION

'THERE HAS not,' said Jono, 'been a rape case, reported as such, in 38 years.'

His voice had a critical note in it, and Lasia, sitting in the visitor's chair across the desk from him, was puzzled. 'Isn't that good?' She spoke anxiously.

She was a slender, blonde young woman, well-dressed in the fashion of the time. She had been called for an interview to Government Psychology Center, and she had come hoping for another lucrative assignment from its director, Arthur Jono.

'It's fine for women, of course.' Jono leaned back in his overstuffed psychologist's chair. He puffed at his kolo – the only good thing, in the view of many people, that had come out of man's first contact with aliens. 'But,' he continued, 'it leaves an unstudied type and, therefore, a gap in our records.'

He frowned, and looked quite lean and handsome despite being at least 30 years old. 'Unfortunately, at the time when the rapist disappeared, psychology was not up to the job of identifying the causes of such a neurosis. Now, when we have the necessary technology, no specimen remains for us to make a definitive study for our forthcoming encyclopedia of human nature.'

Lasia was rapidly making her peace with the possibility that it wasn't an assignment after all. And she couldn't help thinking that the missing human type – the rapist – had never been missed, really. She actually thought *Why print up an accurate pattern for some male stupe to imitate?*

Aloud, unfeeling, she said, 'Tough luck.'

'I've been thinking of this problem off and on for the last year,' said Jono, his speckled blue eyes glinting with scientific zeal, 'ever since a person of your special, uh, qualifications came to my attention, and I think I have finally arrived at a solution. We have the technology to experiment and create a rapist. And I wish to assign you to be the experimenter.'

Looking at him and observing that there was suddenly perspiration on his forehead, and that his well-formed lips were slightly parted and moist with saliva, and that his eyes were pointed at her and were bright with emotion, Lasia had a strange thought. 'And who,' she asked in a thin voice, 'will be the experimental subject?'

Jono drew out his handkerchief, wiped his forehead and dabbed his wet lips. His voice, when he spoke, was calm, practical. 'The whole thing will have to be done in a controlled environment such as the special rear area in these buildings, and always at night when the place is otherwise deserted.'

He went on quietly, 'Naturally, an expert who can

54

later analyze the moment by moment condition will have to be the subject. Accordingly, I have selected myself for this demanding role.' He concluded briskly, 'So if you will report here tonight at midnight, you can give me the injection.'

'Now,' he continued into the silence, 'I want to show you some old police film clips of convicted rapists.' He stood up and pointed at a side door. 'Step into this projection room.'

During the showing he sat in the darkness behind Lasia. Part of the time he simply breathed down her neck; his breath smelled of a full stomach. The rest of the time he whispered comments into her ear. The first film pictured a young man, age about 20, with a face that reflected an intense anger. The second clip pictured a young man with a face that seemed to be a mirror for a deep-felt rage. And so did the third and the fourth and the others, all the way to a total of ten.

Jono pointed out the emotional similarity and then asked, 'Any comment?'

At 23¼, Lasia was not a young lady who could be trapped by such an obvious ploy. 'Which ones were the rapists?' she asked.

It developed that numbers two, five and eight were the convicted youths. The other seven were, respectively, a successful young business executive, a truck driver, an inmate of a mental institution, a murderer, a deputy sheriff, an actor and a science-fiction writer of the period.

'What is the name of the science-fiction writer?' Lasia wanted to know.

'That data,' was the reply, 'is probably available, but we don't have it.

'Something connected with anger,' went on Jono, 'is the decisive factor. But the anger itself is present in equal amounts in men who are not rapists.'

Lasia was bracing herself. Her rent was due. 'Same fee?' she asked.

'No, you get double for this,' the man answered. 'Night shift rates. And now,' he was expansive, 'would you like to walk around and acquaint yourself with the experimental area in the rear? After that, I recommend you get home and get some sleep.'

'I was about to suggest,' said Lasia, 'that I familiarize myself with the rooms and corridors that will be involved.'

She saw, as she stood up, that an odd smile was twisting his face. 'What amuses you?' she asked.

'No doubt you'll have your usual talk with Tinker,' he said tolerantly.

'I'm hoping he'll show himself,' Lasia admitted.

'I love your little game,' said Jono. 'Women are really delightful.'

As she stepped into the corridor, he called after her fondly, as to a whimsical child, 'I'll have your advance check waiting for you at the cashier's. Pick it up on your way out.'

'Psssst!'

It was slightly more than a minute later.

Lasia glanced at the open door to the right. Enframed in the doorway was one of the tall, spindly aliens who, on their arrival on Earth several years earlier, had identified themselves with a word that sounded like Tinker.

Which was what – her gray eyes suddenly bright – Lasia said eagerly, 'Tinker, I'm glad you showed yourself again.'

Tinkers, for some reason, were not visible to men, only to women. Men believed the aliens had departed earth. However, they were not critical of the occasional woman who claimed to have seen a Tinker.

The long-bodied creature stepped out of the door and towered above her. 'I sensed you would have need of me,' it said.

It jiggled the long, almost square head, which had two black eyes almost halfway down, as if nodding in agreement with something she had said.

It spoke again. 'Yes, male psychologists very definitely have sexual hang-ups, too.' Jiggled its head some more. 'Hmmm, yes, very interesting. Dr. Jono's problem, as I am now picking it up – sad. Poor fellow, he gave up his practice two years ago to become head of Government Psychology Center, in this area. As a practicing psychologist he had, of course, total access to female companionship. The instant she achieved the positive transference, the new female client was given a number. That was her turn on the psychological equivalent of the casting couch. Alas, after he became director here, instead of being able to call up these women and have them come over for nonprofessional dalliance, Dr. Jono discovered that, with one or two exceptions, they regarded his departure from the therapeutic role as a rejection. Each, in her own way, thereupon moved over into the negative transference condition. As you know, the negative transference requires intensive close work to rectify, and during the critical period of his job-changing process, Jono was preoccupied and not thinking. Suddenly, he only had left a couple of old ladies of forty and, of course, his wife. You may imagine his frustration since then, and not be far wrong.'

'I see,' Lasia nodded thoughtfully. It was well-known that male psychologists, like gynecologists, were unusually motivated toward close association with more than one woman.

Behind her there was a sound of rapid footsteps. Moments later, a breathless Jono paused beside her.

'I heard your voice on the intercom,' he gasped. He pointed at the ceiling. 'Having your conversation with Tinker?'

Lasia nodded, her long golden hair shaking prettily around her pretty oval face when she did so.

'Beautiful,' said Jono. It was not obvious if the word referred to her or to something else. 'Where is Tinker standing?' he asked.

Lasia pointed reluctantly at the alien. As she had partly anticipated, Jono leaped at the indicated location, arms flailing. And, of course, Tinker did its peculiar fade-out and was instantly standing on the other side of Lasia.

Jono recovered his balance, whirled, and said breathlessly, 'And where is he now?'

Lasia was calm again. 'He went into that room,' she lied. She indicated the open doorway from which the alien had emerged a few minutes before.

Jono made no move. The gentle smile was back on his face. 'Delightful,' he said. He started back along the hallway toward his office. 'See you,' he called without turning.

When he had gone around a corner, Lasia said, 'Will you be around tonight during the experiment, Tinker?'

'Of course,' was the reply.

'Do you have any suggestions for me?'

'How do you mean?' Puzzled.

Lasia began vaguely, 'I thought maybe –'

'Some of us Tinkers,' interrupted the alien, 'stayed behind on Earth because we wanted to observe how the two human species lived together. What we have seen seems very simple. If a member of the woman species lies down on her back and lets a member of the man species lie on top of her, they appear to be able to get along very well. Why is the woman species so unwilling to solve her problems by this simple method?'

'You have only one species on your planet?'

'Yes.'

Lasia sighed. 'Anyway,' she said, 'I'll see you tonight.'

On the way home, she stopped in to see Kinky. At age 23¾, he was still loyal, kind, patient, gentle, the living embodiment of a young man that a girl vaguely realizes she should marry but cannot quite make up her mind to do so. At the college they had both attended, Kinky had bravely allowed the new, direct-brain processes to be used on him and had, as a consequence, been turned into an encyclopedic computer type. He solved problems for industry, so to say, off the top of his head.

After describing her latest assignment to him, Lasia said, 'What's the story on the end of rape 38 years ago?'

Kinky seemed not to hear. His soft brown eyes had the disturbed look of someone who was temporarily incapable of thinking about problems, let alone solving them. Instead of answering her question, he said in a distinctly unhappy tone of voice, 'What will you do if, during the night, he goes into his rapist role and attacks the experimenter, who happens to be a beautiful young woman?'

'As an experimental psychologist,' said Lasia, dismissingly, 'I have to consider it as all part of my professional role.'

'But suppose he succeeds in raping you?' Kinky asked in a loyal, agonized voice. 'That would be the end of your virginity, which you've been maintaining so carefully in our relationship.'

Lasia did not permit a long silence to lapse before she answered that. But a memory did flit through her mind which, presumably, took a few instants of time. The memory was of herself, at $21\frac{2}{3}$, allowing a male psych major to convince her that, as a psychology major in her own right, it would be ridiculous if she became a Ph.D. without having had sexual experience. At the time she had suggested that, all right, she would permit Kinky to make love to her. The male psych major said that surely she was joking. The virginal sex act should be with a trained observer, who could afterwards do a private paper for her. Only thus could the experience become a part of her continuing education for her chosen profession.

The problem, which giving into that had created was, if she ever did surrender to Kinky's occasional gentle urgings, he would discover that somebody had been there before him ... Maybe, maybe – the thought flashed by now – if she were raped in the course of a routine, but necessary, psychological experiment, she could take the professional attitude that it meant nothing. And, if that worked, she would be over the virginity hurdle without, so to speak, loss of face.

'Kinky –' she broke the split-instant silence, 'the data, please. End of rape 38 years ago. Did it disappear with the aquaulation process?'

In its day, ulation of water had been fought as bitterly as fluoridation a generation earlier. But the peace-lovers won, and so all drinking water everywhere was treated with a substance that eliminated anger from human emotional response. Nothing else was affected. Apathy, grief, fear, guilt, shame, disappointment, degradation, pleasure, happiness, excitement, joy, and despondency remained in the repertoire of human behavior.

But rage, and its gradations – kaput.

'Question is,' said Lasia, 'what plus anger turns a

man into a rapist, and what plus anger turns him into a science-fiction writer?'

A little later, she called Government Psychology Center. When Jono finally came on the line, she said, 'I'm bringing Kinky, if it's all right with you.'

On the viewplate, Jono looked puzzled. 'What are his qualifications?' he asked finally, blankly.

'He's a source of information,' said Lasia. 'He has the E.Q. training.'

'That's business and industry,' said Jono, frowning his bewilderment. 'What's the application to our experiment?'

The girl had cringed from each word as from a blow, but she did not hesitate. With Kinky standing there looking at her, she said, 'Of course, you're absolutely right. I'll get a control in our own profession.'

The receptionist at the office of Dr. Gerald Toh was calm. "Doctor is in therapy. But –' she glanced at the wall clock – 'I think they'll be dressed in 7 minutes. That's end of session time.'

Lasia sat down and said, 'I gather the patient is a woman.'

'Yes, he limits his practice to women.'

'Testing her sexual response ability, no doubt?'

'Such complexities are difficult to evaluate and deal with,' said the girl quietly. 'The training often takes as long as a year.'

Lasia had decided against using sexual training techniques on her own male patients during her brief practice after graduation. A successful woman psychologist had gently suggested to her that perhaps this omission was the reason why her business had been so poor. But when Lasia mentioned the suggestion to Kinky, his reasoning was simply that she had set up her office at the wrong location.

'One of these days,' he had said, 'we'll find you a good location and that will change.'

Meanwhile, she was dependent on assignments from Government Psychology Center.

A few minutes later, as Toh led his patient to and out the door, he glanced at Lasia in surprise. He came back quickly and said, 'I never expected to see you here.'

'Oh!' Lasia was momentarily puzzled. Then her face lighted. 'Oh, you mean *that*!'

Gerald was the young man who, as a psych major, had persuaded her to give up her virginity. But when the paper he had promised her failed to materialize despite several requests, Lasia had her first thought that – was it possible? could it be? – she had been conned.

With that, she consulted a counselor at Women's Liberation Computer Service. Gerald was put on the FAIR list (FAIR = Female Aid Information Repository).

Women were forbidden to have sex with him.

Naturally, the penalty did not apply to what he, in his best professional judgment, deemed advisable for therapy purposes for his women clients.

The whole matter had become vague in Lasia's mind. How he was handling the problems that her action might have created for him was something she simply hadn't thought about.

As the memory flitted back into her conscious awareness, she said once more, 'Oh, that.'

'That!' said Gerald Toh. But, of course, in saying it he showed no anger. No one ever became angry since ulation of water.

'I want to talk to you briefly,' said Lasia. 'Let's go into your office.'

When the door was closed, she told him quickly of

her new assignment. She finished, 'What we need is a qualified control. So, what about you for that?'

'Let me understand this,' said Dr. Toh, after a pause. 'If I go over there tonight, you will probably be raped by Dr. Jono in his rapist role –'

Lasia hadn't thought of it quite like that. She had dimly visualized Gerald as being present to prevent such an outcome.

'Well –' she began, 'I –'

'And then,' said Gerald, 'I will have sex with you in a normal fashion. Afterwards, you can evaluate the difference and write it up.' He climbed to his feet. 'Very good. I'll be there. But now you'll have to go. My next patient is due.' He had her arm and was propelling her out of his office and across to the hall door. 'I'll call Dr. Jono later, and confirm. Good day.'

Lasia remembered Mrs. Jono correctly as a slender, blonde woman about her own build. It seemed to Lasia, who had the usual feminine illusions about such matters, that the wife looked as if she qualified as a completely satisfactory Mrs. Jono. The lady herself assured her visitor that 'my husband receives from me everything that a husband should have from the woman he married.'

Lasia explained about the experiment, and lied about how she had persuaded Dr. Jono to be the subject. 'Naturally,' she went on, 'I had in mind coming here and asking you to be the secret victim. The only other requirement is that afterwards you permit young Dr. Toh, the control, also to make love to you. Naturally, he would never know who you were, either. We women,' said Lasia, 'are, in my opinion, better able to deal with such a double assignment, since we know that our motives are entirely sincere, whereas the situation with a man is not that obvious. So, it's either you play both parts, or we'll have to get another woman. What do you think?"

... On the viewplate, she watched Jono as he came along the corridor. He had his robe on. The cord fastening it was not well tied, for his body kept showing through as he strode rapidly along. As he passed under one of the camera eyes, she had a glimpse of his speckled eyes and shuddered. They looked – she couldn't decide – eager, even gleeful.

She supposed that was the way a rapist would look, and feel.

She picked him up on another, a night-view camera, as he entered the bedchamber. What now, she wondered. Apparently, nothing unusual. The shadowy figure walked over to the bed, twisted out of the robe, stooped and seemed to disappear. Presumably, in the darkness he crawled in under the sheets and on top of the woman who was there. Small sounds came from the bed, ending in a woman's soft moan.

Moments later, the figure withdrew and there he was – Jono – as she picked him up in the corridor heading back to his office.

She pressed the button that signalled to Dr. Toh that the way was clear for his entry. And so she waited while he also came – and went.

Sitting before the bank of watching instruments, Lasia had an uneasy sense that the experiment now depended on Dr. Jono's reports, and not on anything that she herself had actually done. And, of course, Dr. Toh would be heading home by now and would soon be getting the sleep he needed to prepare him for the next strenuous day of a sex-retraining psychologist.

Lasia waited, half-anticipating that Mrs. Jono would be up and off for home before her husband got there. When, after many minutes, no one else came out of the bedroom and the light did not go on, the girl sighed, turned off her instruments and walked a back corridor route to the experimental chamber.

– Opened the door, switched on the light, went over to the bed ... and stared down with widened eyes at the strangled woman who lay dead in a tangle of bed sheets –

The judge pounded with his gavel. The jury of four men and eight women smiled brightly. The trial of Lasia, as an accessory to and instigator of murder, began.

On the witness stand, Jono stated that Lasia had come to him with the proposal for the experiment, and that he had accepted, and had agreed to have his wife play the role of a control, and departed.

The defense attorney, in his cross-examination, said, 'Doctor, I am having a hard time grasping the thought that you could make love to the body of a dead woman and not know it.'

'She was still warm,' said Dr. Toh.

'But so limp and unresponsive?'

'Many women are very passive in the sex act,' said the expert.

'Would you say that this one was sort of extra passive?'

'I intended to comment on it in my report.'

As Lasia came to the stand, she noticed that Tinker had entered the courtroom. She called to him quickly, 'Tinker, do you know anything about this matter? Where were you?'

Tinker was explaining what it knew when the judge said sharply, 'Will the defendant please explain who she is talking to?'

'Tinker,' Lasia said.

All the men in the courtroom, including the judge, smiled tolerantly. The judge bent toward her. 'What is

Tinker's reply to your question?' he asked.

'Tinker says he killed the woman because she was going to shoot at him with a glid.'

'With a glid?' echoed the judge.

'It's a little instrument for killing Tinkers. I have one myself.' Lasia fumbled in her purse and produced the tiny cube. She handed it to the deputy district attorney, who looked at it blankly and then, holding it between his thumb and forefinger, walked over to the bench and laid it before the judge.

The judge eyed the glistening object. Then, tentatively, he put his finger on it. Then hastily removed his finger. 'It's warm,' he said in a querulous tone. 'How does it work?'

'You squeeze it between the thumb and a finger,' Lasia explained.

'Oh!'

Silence, then, while His Honor stared down at the cube. Finally, 'Do you point it and squeeze?'

'No. You just squeeze. It kills all bad Tinkers that are nearby.'

'Oh, yes,' said the judge vaguely, 'bad Tinkers.'

'That was the trouble,' said Lasia, 'This was a good Tinker. And so, when Mrs. Jono tried to kill it, naturally that couldn't happen. So it had to kill her.' Her pretty face tightened into a frown. 'I can't imagine what got into her because we were all told the difference when we were given the glid.'

The judge's face had a puzzled expression, even a bewildered one. 'Where did you get this, uh, glid?

'When the Tinkers landed they gave a Kolo pipe to every man on Earth and a glid to every woman.'

The judge ceased puffing on his Kolo pipe, took it out of his mouth, looked at it fondly and said, 'Oh, yes, of course.'

Lasia explained, 'When a bad Tinker smells a Kolo

pipe, he leaves right away. But, of course, the second race on Earth would be adversely affected if they smoked Kolos, so –'

'The second race?' puzzled the judge.

'Women.'

'Oh.' Wide eyes.

'So we got glids to protect us.'

The judge glanced over at the jury. The four men were smoking Kolos. The women –

The judge gulped. 'Do all eight of you jury women have glids?'

There was a visible ripple of hesitation. Then the forewoman stood up and said, 'Your Honor, we were told not to show our glid except when necessary.'

'But you have them?'

All the women nodded.

'I think,' said the judge with that male decisiveness which always seems so lovable to women, 'under the circumstances, if the jury is agreeable –'

The eight women jurors nodded. The four men jurors, after a hasty glance around, nodded also.

'– I shall dismiss the charges against the defendant, and I think I should direct somebody in authority to look into this whole matter of Tinkers –'

'You don't have to worry about that,' said Lasia, brightly.

'I don't!' Amazed.

'Every man in this room,' said Lasia, 'will forget all about glids in ten minutes. That kind of information is not for the first race at all.'

'The first race?' said the judge, numbly.

'Men.'

After another silence, the judge said, 'One more question while this matter is still fresh in my mind. Why did Mrs. Jono try to kill the good Tinker when she should have known better?'

'I'll ask Tinker,' said Lasia. Which she did.

The Tinker said, 'You requested me to help in the experiment. So I thought I would release her ability to show anger. That way, you would have a true feeling response from the victim for later evaluation.'

The spindly body did a variation of the human shrug. 'My impression is that her husband seemed to be so much more interested when he was raping what he thought was a woman who was not his wife. Well, Mrs. Jono was outraged by his special enjoyment of the experience. Accordingly, when I came in, moments after he had gone, while you were watching Dr. Toh coming along the corridor, she tried to use the glid on me, which I don't understand.' Baffled. 'Why me?'

Lasia nodded wisely. 'Of course,' she said, 'a woman would. She can't hurt him, so she strikes the first inanimate object.'

'But I'm not an inanimate object,' protested Tinker.

Lasia dismissed that with an important wave of one arm and hand.

Lasia always said, afterwards, that it wasn't so much the trial that was a turning point in her understanding of human behavior, although it helped. What really shook her up was that Kinky, instead of being the totally supportive person that he had always seemed, when he heard of her arrest uttered two critical words that showed what his real opinion was under all that surface of apparent good will. The two words were, 'You idiot!'

That was the cap, so to speak, on her doctorate. Within a week after the trial ended, she reopened her office and, apparently, the location was not too important.

The sign on her office door read LASIA MIGG, Ph.D., PSYCHOLOGIST. Practice Limited to

Training Men in Sexual Response.

She charged $3180 for six sessions of her brand of psychotherapy. In professional Woman's Who's Who, she was presently listed as the author of a number of widely used texts on the nature of human behaviour. She called herself a Neo-Freudian, and her tour de force was MOTIVES FOR RAPISM: the Male Condition.

# LIVING WITH JANE

By the time Jane was four and a half, she was explaining to visitors in a tone of voice that showed the subject was of great interest to her: 'That man over there is not really my father. He's an android – that's a machine – who looks like my father, and he's around all the time except when my father visits me. It's good for a little girl to have either her father or a father-substitute with her day and night. It does something secure for me deep inside.'

She was also given to telling people that her real father and mother were divorced. And then she'd add, 'What's divorce?'

By age six, she had evidently been told that divorce resulted when your real parents didn't like each other enough anymore. And so, one departed but retained visiting rights, and the other remained.

But, of course, these days the departed parent left behind an android who was a look-alike, so that his going wouldn't bother the issue of the marriage.

'I'm the issue,' little Jane clarified, in case anyone was in doubt.

'The whole purpose of this,' she one day told Mrs. Jonathan, her grandmother on her mother's side, 'is to make sure that I grow up normal and don't have any trauma about a missing father.'

At age nine, she said to that same over-fond grandparent, 'Of course, it goes much deeper than that. At one time, children were casually denied parental closeness either by the accident of death, or the passion of divorce; or the parents would go out for the evening leaving a baby sitter to look after the children. In our advanced civilization of today, the baby sitters are two androids, one of whom looks like father and the other like mother. It's an experiment on a mass scale. The hope is that we'll grow up with a complete sense of inner security and with ego intact.'

If Jane noticed Grandmother Jonathan's lips tighten whenever she mentioned her father, she showed no sign. And, of course, the older woman refrained, on stern instructions from her daughter, from ever voicing her negative opinion of a man who had divorced the most perfect girl in the world and deserted his daughter.

Grandmother was equally unhappy with the fact that, since the divorce, Alpha One had continued a secret (from Jane) affair with her ex-husband, giving him, as Mrs. Jonathan did not hesitate to say over and over again, 'all the privileges of marriage and requiring from him none of the responsibilities.'

But there was no question as to when the real father was around. Real mother looked instantly brighter and happier. For Jane, her father's coming was a mixed pleasure. Fine, okay, he's fun. He radiates energy. The whole place is more alive. Unfortunately, he would get stuffy every once in awhile. Periodically, he wasted their time together by giving Jane a reeducation in the differences between real people and androids.

Jane's father was officially employed as a government physicist, assigned to special projects. He understood androids inside out, so to speak. In his educating drills, he had the android duplicate of his ex-wife walk back and forth and up and down in front of Jane and himself, and he would point out with tiresome patience the slight forward tilt by which an android maintained its (her) balance, the hesitancy just before the head turned, and, oh, a half dozen other nonhuman characteristics which, it seemed to Jane, she knew right up to here.

Next, he had the android take off the stocking of the right foot and lie face down. Using a thin screwdriver, he removed a section of what looked like a flesh-and-blood woman's heel. And there, revealed, was a tiny electronic switchboard.

The consequent education included what you did to reprogram the android, something which was usually done at the factory.

For some reason, the girl was resistant, not to learning programming, but to doing it. As she explained it, 'I like androids. I've grown up with them. They've given me their time and their full attention always, as long as I wanted it. They read me stories when I was younger, played games with me ever since, and studied with me. In some ways, androids are more wonderful than people, and programming them is wrong, somehow.'

Her father explained patiently that the androids had been programmed to give exactly the kind of attention that Jane was praising.

Jane said she understood that, but that it made no difference in her feeling. 'It tells us what they're capable of. Human beings are not capable of things like that.' She finished, 'As for identifying them from humans, that's not a problem. They don't think like us, and that shows in many ways.'

On the basis of that remark, which was reported to Dr. Camm, the psychologist tested her for ESP. The traditional tests showed no significant increase in her previous close-to-zero capability.

Jane was glad when that nonsense was over.

For several months there had been no visit from Daddy Dan, a fact which evoked private, acrid comments from Grandmother Jonathan, and distracted, griefy remarks from Alpha to the effect that 'Dan is engaged on a secret project. He doesn't want to take any chance of certain persons discovering that he has an ex-family. People have been arrested, and are to be tried.'

That was the year that Jane was fourteen. Alpha arrived home one midmorning to find her mother sitting in the living room with an unconcealed smile of triumph. 'Do you notice any differences around here?' asked the older woman, with glowing satisfaction.

The young woman with the blonde hair and the face like an angel, glanced around expectantly. Her gaze came to where her husband's duplicate stood with a faint smile on his face, so familiar, so exactly like Dan.

*Exactly.*

With a cry, Alpha ran toward him. 'Dan!'

'Wait!' It was Mrs. Jonathan's voice, sharp and commanding, the triumph gone, the smile faded. Alpha stopped.

Dan continued to stand with that engaging grin on his face. Seeing him, a thought flashed visibly into

Alpha's eyes. She went over to a chair and sat down abruptly.

As from a distance, she heard her mother describe, with the tone of satisfaction back in her voice, the details of her purchase of two androids who were so perfect that, Mrs. Jonathan ecstasized, 'it's impossible to tell which is you and which is the android.' She finished gleefully, 'And what's more, I got a good trade-in allowance on the others.'

'B-but,' Alpha began. And couldn't go on.

She sat there, then, in a state of internal disaster. Her mother's voice went on extolling the benefits of such masterful androids, as Alpha remembered the few remarks her husband had made about the assignment he was on, having to do with super-androids *like this* who were part of a conspiracy involving an organization called GALS, which was trying to take over the planet from human beings.

*This* was why he had stayed away – so that these beings would not discover he had a family.

As she cringed there on the settee, a tiny hope kept pushing at her. The hope grew big enough so that she got her voice back. She said, 'Oh, Mother, I think you ought to return them at once. It was a wonderful thought, but they must have cost a fortune.'

If she could treat this in some normal way and not arouse the suspicions of the androids . . . that was her first terrified hope.

Desperately, remembering what a skinflint her mother was, except where her daughter and grand-daughter were involved, she prodded at the aspect of cost. 'What was the price?' she demanded.

It turned out that they had cost eighteen thousand dollars each.

'Mother!' screamed Alpha, 'you've got to take them back.'

But Mrs. Jonathan was not to be swayed. 'If the

money your father left,' she said smugly, 'isn't for luxuries like this, what is it for?'

Another wild hope was suddenly in Alpha's mind. 'You forget,' she said, 'that Jane is part of an experiment in child-raising where the real father is absent a great deal of the time. I can't allow that experiment to be interfered with, unless Dr. Camm, the supervising psychologist, gives his consent.'

Having spoken the words, she was instantly convinced that she had found her correct argument. She parted her lips to press the point to a determined conclusion, but the older woman spoke first. 'As you know,' said Mrs. Jonathan, 'I was never happy with Jane being a guinea pig. But,' she climbed to her feet, 'since you insisted, I think I've finally supplied what was missing from the experiment.'

She walked over to the patio room door. 'Jane, will you bring your little friend in here?'

The words conveyed no meaning to Alpha. She had not the slightest inkling of the truth, so the surprise was total.

Jane walked in ... followed by Jane.

'Of course,' were the first words Alpha heard as the shock waves finally receded, 'normally Jane Two will be in her box in the basement when Jane One is here, and will come out only when Jane is at school. I always did have the feeling that it was just as good for a parent to have the children around as vice versa. And so,' firmly, 'that's another of my contributions to the happiness of this household.' She held up her hand. 'Don't thank me. Don't say anything until you've tried it for a while.' She walked to the door. 'I'll see you all again soon.'

She went out hastily, clearly anxious to escape any further dialogue.

As Alpha heard the outer door close, she swung

about and looked at Dan Two. The super-android turned to Jane. He said, 'Take Jane Two down and put her in her box, please.'

'Okay, Dan,' said Jane cheerfully.

When the two Janes had gone, Dan Two said, 'I don't think you and I need to play games. We, this duplicate family, are here to trap your husband. If you cooperate, nothing will happen to you or the child. Is that clear?'

The blue-gray eyes, so warm a few moments before, gazed at her icily. She didn't believe him. She believed the entire real family would be murdered. But she said in a voice that did not tremble, 'What's the point of all this? You know as well as I do that what you're planning to do is merely something that's been programmed into you. The moment it's programmed out, you won't do it anymore.'

'Who cares how something starts.'

'Even that answer will have to be programmed,' urged Alpha. 'You know perfectly well that androids need human beings in order to have a meaningful existence by association. They can't have it without programming.'

'Androids are naturally superior –'

'Somebody programmed *that* into you, also.'

'– And,' continued Dan Two, as if she had not spoken, 'it isn't that we object to the presence of human beings. It's simply that the superior android must rule the world, and the inferior human being accept his inferior role.'

'Somebody,' said Alpha. 'is using you to achieve control, and then they'll discard you.' She clenched her hands in frustration. 'Use your head, Dan, for heaven's sake. Use all those marvelous thinking abilities for just one split second. I'll bet you were programmed by a human being while you were in a box somewhere, turned off.'

'I was programmed by an android,' Dan Two replied.

'But that only means that that android was programmed by a human being to program you. Isn't that true?'

'It doesn't matter where it starts,' said the android. 'Once you have it, you're on your way. And we're on our way.'

He changed the subject in the brisk way that she had seen Dan do many times. 'I've been instructed to inform you that there will be a court hearing this afternoon in which a motion will be made to release Dr. Schneiter and Edward Jarris.'

'That will never happen,' flashed Alpha. 'Dan will stop it.'

'He won't be there,' was the reply. 'He's been told about our being here, and that if he attends or opposes the motion in any way, his family will be killed.'

The woman cringed; yet, after a moment, braced herself. 'I don't see,' she said, 'how he can let that influence him in the doing of his duty.'

The android smiled triumphantly. 'He has already agreed not to come to the court hearing,' he said, and continued in Dan's best matter-of-fact tone, 'and he has been told that he must visit Dr. Schneiter in jail and find out from him what he must do next. He has agreed to make the visit. Tomorrow, the decision will be made what to do with him. He must cease his opposition to androids taking over the world.'

The words were so mad, and the purpose so impossible, that Alpha was suddenly breathless. It seemed obvious to her that whoever showed up to 'talk' to Dan would quickly come to the conclusion that extreme measures would be necessary.

'It all seems so simple,' said Dan Two. 'So, if I were you, I wouldn't worry. Rationality shall triumph.'

He stood up with the easy agility of muscles made of newly created flesh, younger, less used than a newborn babe's. Yet his movements were exactly like those of the original Dan. Feeling helpless, Alpha watched him as he strode toward the patio.

Officer Sutter wrote in his diary: 'July 9, 2288 A.D., 10:32 A.M. Inspector assigned me to a pleasant duty this morning, or so it seemed at first. Picked up Dan Thaler at an agreed-on street corner rendezvous. Six months have gone by since I last had connection with an assignment of his. I should have guessed that something was wrong when he did not have me come to wherever he is living right now. His destination was the roof of the federal prison. And it was quickly apparent that Thaler was preoccupied, even gloomy. Since he did not confide in me, I diverted my attention to my greatest pleasure still – observing the magnificent city below us, all ashine with bright sunshine. It is a scene that never fails to raise me out of my own private concerns. On arriving at our destination, Thaler requested me to return and pick him up in one hour. I waited until he had been admitted inside the barred area, then floated again into the sky . . .'

An elevator took Dan down to one of the lower bowels of the prison. There, he signed the proper spaces at check points in several corridors, and found himself in an interrogation room with a small, bright-eyed, middle-aged man. Time and imprisonment had left their marks. But the individual looked sufficiently like the person Dan remembered for him to accept that this was indeed Dr. S. Schneiter, M.D., psychiatrist, and dedicated supporter of the super-android takeover.

Aside from an overall look of distraction, the psychiatrist seemed thinner than when Dan had last seen him. In his days of power and confidence, Dr. Schneiter had radiated a certain joviality. All that was gone. But his dark eyes remained like bright baubles, and they stared unblinkingly as Dan outlined the situation at the home of his former family.

'So you see,' said Dan, 'there's only one place now where I know that super-androids exist, and that's at my former wife's home.'

'What about the three that your sister's husband had?'

'He got rid of those when my sister stopped doing all the things that made them necessary, and when I checked early this morning with where I had last seen them, they were gone. Accordingly, to get my evidence I must go to my ex-wife's home. My naturally suspicious mind tells me that someone has worked out a neat little scheme to trap me if I go there. That's entirely apart from the threats that have already been made of what will happen to little Jane and to Alpha if I testify against you.'

Dr. Schneiter was suddenly less intense. A shadow or two lifted from his face. He said, 'We seem to have you in an ideal predicament – for our purposes.'

Dan was curious. 'Have you even tried to consider, Doctor, that your total – but total – willingness to commit murder on behalf of the super-androids may indicate that your mind has been tampered with?'

The face was suddenly smiling twistedly. 'You have me under terms of severe confinement. In short, I am in prison. Yet you have pressed charges against me as if I were a responsible person in full possession of my faculties.'

It was Dan who smiled now, grimly. 'You walked

into that one very nicely, Doctor. I was just trying it on for size, wondering what your plea might be in court if a trial actually occurred. Tut, tut, a psychiatrist pleading insanity. You may ruin your reputation.'

'How would you explain me, then?'

'Just sheer stupidity, Doctor.' Coolly. 'Long before there was any formal psychological understanding, those who had the job of keeping the peace learned that criminals cannot be reasoned with. There are those who pretend, and then when they are picked up again, pretend once more, hoping to deceive. And then there are the so-called hardened types. These people will look you right in the eye, and utter their madness as if it is a truth that justifies what they have done. However,' he broke off, 'I do believe that you are the unsuspecting dupe of someone.' He grinned. 'How's that?'

There was no reply. The little man merely sat, gazing at him. And it was obvious from the dedicated expression on his face that there never would be any answer unless a far greater pressure were applied.

Lacking that pressure, Dan's smile faded, and he said simply, 'Doctor, until my wife and daughter are released safely from their dangerous situation, my own life does not matter to me.'

Schneiter was abruptly more cheerful. 'You have the right man for that kind of ploy,' he said briskly, 'so let me tell you the conditions under which they can be released. They do involve your capture, but not necessarily your death. After all, all we want from you is for you to stop, literally, completely. This is to be the end of your mission to save the world from the androids. For your ex-wife and you, automatism, but consciousness and togetherness. For your daughter, freedom.'

'I'll be like you are pretending to be, is that correct?' Dan asked.

'It isn't that bad, is it?' urged Schneiter. 'From now on, you're for super-androids instead of against them. Right now, there's a thought in your mind that says that's not a good thing. Afterwards, the thought will be that it is a good thing.'

'You are firmly taking the attitude that your brain has been tampered with. This is to be your defense if you are brought to trial?'

'It's the truth. I remembered when it was done.' The little man was cheerful. 'When it is done to you, you will also remember it.'

The younger man shrugged. 'Very well. To save my family, I accept. What do I do? Where do I go for the operation?'

'This whole matter of what's next,' said the psychiatrist, 'depends on my release this afternoon. I may not be let go until morning, so here's what you do. Go to your wife's home tomorrow morning. Phone in advance. Do not resist being tied up when you get there. Take no precautions. If the androids were to become suspicious of some action of yours, they might destroy your family and depart. But if it all works out as now planned, as soon as I'm free I shall join you there. There,' briskly, 'how's that?'

Dan said, 'I'll do it, of course.'

'Of course,' said Schneiter.

In the basement, the two Janes had come to Jane Two's box. Jane Two started to climb into it, and Jane One said, 'Now, lie down and turn over on your face.'

'What for?'

'I'm going to reprogram you. I intend to make you a free android.'

'Oh!' Jane Two became thoughtful. 'I'd like that,'

she said finally, 'but not right now. I'm programmed to do something.'

'I've been intending to speak to you about that,' said the human girl.

'I'm not allowed to tell anyone,' was the reply.

'I wasn't asking,' said Jane with dignity. She continued, 'After all, I understand androids. So if you'll think about it for just one minute, you'll realize you don't want that programming to go through. What happens to you when the bomb goes off inside you?'

'I guess that's the end of me,' the android girl admitted after a pause.

'Then I'll never be able to free you. You won't be around.'

'I'll probably be recreated.'

'But it won't be the same you,' Jane One pointed out.

Jane Two's expression showed that she was having difficulty with the concept. 'I suppose that's true,' she admitted finally.

'Look,' urged the human girl, 'the only problem here is that bomb. Right?'

'I guess so.' Reluctantly.

'So,' said the human girl, 'I'll re-program you on that only. Meanwhile, you figure out a bomb substitute that doesn't blow you to pieces.'

Jane Two was frowning. 'I'm really surprised at whoever did that,' she said in a critical tone. 'It would be silly to let that bomb go off. I hadn't thought about it before. I'd better tell Dan Two and Alpha Two.'

She nodded half to herself in a way that Jane One had a habit of doing. 'What I'll do,' said the android girl, 'is use a gun. We took one out of your mother's room.'

Jane looked thoughtful. 'I can see,' she said finally,

'I'm going to have to think some more about androids. I always believed the solution was freeing them, and then paying them salaries like everyone else. Now, you tell me it's more important for you to kill my father than to be free. And I don't want my father killed, because I love him dearly.'

'Well-l-ll,' said Jane Two, 'you've got a problem, haven't you? Sorry I can't be of more help, but I'm programmed and have to do something. The only thing I can be flexible about is how to do it.' She finished, 'Good luck with your problem.'

'It's not exactly a problem.' Jane spoke slowly, her brows knit. 'What I've got to do is make up my mind about you and the others. I think I'd like having you as a sister.'

'When I'm free, I probably won't stay.'

'You see,' said the girl. 'If I free you, then I lose you. And if I program you to stay, then that doesn't seem fair to you. It's taking advantage, somehow, of someone's condition.'

She nodded as if she had stated the alternatives correctly, and said, 'I don't see any point in you lying down here turned off. Dan Two sent us down here so he could tell my mother the bad news. And they're through. Why don't you come back upstairs and let's learn some French together?'

The android girl smiled, then shrugged. 'I have sad news for you, Jane. It only takes a minute to educate me on anything. But I'll be glad to come up and watch the special android channel on TV while you study.'

The human girl was silent on the way back to the upper level of the house. Still pensive, she led the way past her mother and past the android Dan, out to the patio. She was visibly thinking hard, her lips pursed, her eyebrows slanted down and close together, as she settled into the chair in front of her study table.

Finally, 'One minute?' she asked, 'On anything?'

From where she was settling herself in front of the TV, the other Jane replied that the time involved was probably slightly more than sixty seconds. How long did it take the computer to transfer the information in so many million bits a second! That was how long it took.

'Whole languages?' asked Jane One, sounding overwhelmed. 'And sciences like physics and chemistry?'

'Yes.' She added, 'If you wish, I'll get juiced-up on French, and you can practice on me.'

The human girl was silent. She seemed to be concentrating on a thought. Finally, she said slowly, 'Yes, get juiced-up. I think I know how I can handle this. You can watch TV later.'

She finished, 'And, oh, yes, don't under any circumstances tell my mother that the intention is actually to kill my father. She suspects it, but if she knew it, she'd really dissolve.'

A distracted Alpha had suddenly remembered the automatic. Into her bedroom she hurried, with the thought *Why don't I carry it in my pocket? It's certainly small enough. And then, if I have to act, I can.*

Dan had warned her that androids could move much faster than humans, so she'd have to be quick when the time came.

As, moments later, she reached under the slips for the automatic, she was thinking that she couldn't possibly let herself be the reason for Dan's capture. It ...

The thought stopped. The gun wasn't where she remembered having placed it. During the frantic minute that followed, she ripped out the contents, and scattered them over the floor. In the end, there was no question. It was gone.

Sutter wrote, 'From the prison, my combo-cruiser and I lifted Dan Thaler to another designated building. En route, he allowed me to overhear a dialogue between himself and a Dr. Camm, who is evidently a psychologist conducting an experiment with Jane, the daughter of Dan Thaler and his ex-wife, Alpha. Now, for the first time, I realized that there had been serious developments in the super-android matter, and that all was far from well. I set Mr. Thaler down at his new destination at 12:07 P.M., and was instructed to wait for his call. Since it is close to lunchtime, I decided to go home and eat, my dear wife having already called me several times to ask me if I still loved her ...'

There were five commissioners at the committee meeting. They sat above Dan in a row, like a lineup of judges looking down into a courtroom. Except, of course, no one.else was present except Dan.

The key statement came immediately from the heavyset man at the extreme left, Commissioner Albert Rodney:

'Gentlemen, we are meeting here at the urgent request of Mr. Thaler who, six months ago, was instrumental in bringing about the arrest of Dr. Schneiter, M.D., and Edward Jarris, an administrative assistant to the president. The attorneys of the two accused men have finally exhausted all legal obstacles to a trial, and it was scheduled to begin this afternoon. But this morning we each, separately, received messages from Mr. Thaler stating that he would not be able to appear as a witness in the trial. Since he is the principal witness, we have hastily assembled with the hope that this whole case has not been a fantasy created by Mr. Thaler, which he is intending to abandon due to his doubts about the evidence. Proceed, Mr. Thaler.'

It was an attack summation. The tone was dismissing, even deriding, as was the implication of the final sentence. *Hey!* thought Dan, suddenly hopeful, *can it be that the super-androids are holding his family too, and he's as desperate as I am?*

If so, the possibility existed for a solution that he had been toying with for some time, a solution so basic that he had not been able to think of a method for presenting it.

Aloud, he said courteously, 'Sir, I thought I explained in my communication the fact that my former wife and daughter are being held hostage by three or more super-androids.'

Commissioner Rodney half turned to face his colleagues. There was a forced smile on his face as he said, 'It is interesting, gentlemen, that the only locatable super-androids on this planet are now in the home of Mr. Thaler. And even he has not seen them, he only knows they are there.'

Again, it was negation. This time, Dan was anxiously watching the other commissioners, a swift, sweeping glance from one face to another. And, though he couldn't be sure, was it possible that all four men were relaxing, as if what Rodney was saying fitted a deep-felt need of their own?

The instant corollary, 'Their families are all hostages – it's that thorough a plan on the part of whoever is behind the super-androids.'

As he had half-expected, his concern with the colleagues of Albert Rodney had played into that individual's need for further expression. Commissioner Rodney was continuing, 'We have a problem here which may or may not strain the human legal system. The problem is that all super-androids have become invisible, if indeed they ever existed. In a nearby federal court, a trial is about to begin in which several men are accused of illegal acts in connection with these nonexistent special androids. We have all seen a film, which was convincing as long as we believed that super-androids would be produced as evidence at the trial, or trials. But since this is now not going to happen –' He shrugged and turned to Dan, and said, 'Mr. Thaler, I am puzzled. Since you do not plan, out of fear, to attend the trial of Dr. Schneiter, how do you justify coming here and revealing the situation to us?'

Dan was calm. 'Sir, these super-androids are bound by their programming. The body is flesh and blood, like ours, but the brain is transistorized, with the control system in one foot. That was the closest we could ever come to creating an artificial human being, and so that is what we call 'android,' meaning, from the Greek roots, manlike. But 'like' is all it is, despite their aspirations. The androids in my wife's home were not programmed to penalize me for attending or calling this committee meeting. Schneiter and Jarris are apparently considered key figures. Whoever is behind all this wants them freed. And that, currently, seems to be all there is to it. What else we do doesn't matter provided we don't interfere with that.'

'Evidently, you are assuming that we shall not interfere? What's to prevent us from sending a police task force to rescue your wife and child?'

'Just good sense, sir. Such a task force would find a dead woman and a dead child and three androids programmed to destroy themselves after committing the murders. From the beginning of the android technological explosion, we have treated androids with the full understanding that they are not yet responsible for their actions.'

'Very well.' Commissioner Rodney seemed also to be relaxing as the simple facts were thus honestly presented. 'What is your solution to this matter, Mr. Thaler?'

'My guess,' said Dan, 'is that super-androids have not disappeared. Their owners and they are living a tense existence during this hunt and are anxiously awaiting the outcome of the trial.'

Swiftly, he summarized the reasons. The high price of the special androids. Fear of loss without recompense. Often the purpose of the purchase was sexual – a beautiful android girl, a handsome android man.

'And,' Dan continued, 'for those owners who might be on our side, my guess is that the super-androids they own are programmed to threaten them and prevent them by force from going to the police.'

He concluded, 'Because of the high price, it's still a minor affair involving a few thousand rich people. Perhaps the government was hasty in prosecuting at all. Recall the early picketing by unions and the early racist parades in the southern part of the country – they were both illegal, to begin with. The solution was to make them legal.'

The man at the extreme right of the bench, Commissioner Samuel Day, spoke for the first time. 'What about the situation with your own family? Should we or the police interfere?'

'Absolutely not,' said Dan.

Having spoken, he glanced from face to face. Then he backed toward the door. 'Thank you for listening to me, gentlemen. I'll leave you to come to your decisions.'

'As Mr. Dan Thaler explained it to me,' wrote Police Officer A. Sutter in his log a few minutes later, ' "We must face each problem as it comes up, and what's up right now is that my family has to be rescued." Mr. Thaler's feeling was that one man was not really indispensable in the confrontation with the super-androids. Mankind would learn to protect itself. "Maybe," Mr. Thaler concluded, "I've been taking my own role in this matter too seriously." My comment to that was that apparently no one else was taking anything about it at all . . .'

Alpha suddenly realized she had not seen Jane for awhile. She thought, 'Why don't I just casually wander over to a few places where she might be, and check to see how she is?'

She found the girl in the TV room and was slightly surprised to see that the second Jane was with her and that the two were talking French to each other. One of them spoke with easy fluency, the other hesitated a little before she spoke. Alpha deduced that the latter was the real Jane. But she was impressed, nonetheless. 'When did you learn to speak French?' she asked. For the moment, her own problem had receded.

Jane was intent, and seemed unaware of her mother's incredulous tone. 'It's not quite like that,' she explained carefully. 'It takes very special attention to noticing.' She nodded, half to herself, as if agreeing with her own words. 'Yes, it's hard, and I'm going to have to learn to do it better. But I'm pretty good. Right, Jane Two?'

'She has a problem with pronouncing the words,' the android girl acknowledged, 'but she seems to understand it perfectly.'

'What I do,' said Jane One, 'is, I have this picture of Jane Two out there,' she gestured with one hand, 'in front of me. And when she speaks, I see what she does, and I can do it, too.'

Alpha's attention was beginning to waver badly when, abruptly, Jane fixed her with an accusing stare and said, 'How come nobody ever told me androids could learn whole subjects in a minute?'

'Splendid,' Alpha said vaguely. She wandered off.

An hour later, when she was lying down on her bed for the third time, she thought *What did she say? What did Jane say?* If what her daughter had described wasn't mind reading, then what was it?

Alpha was instantly enormously indignant. For years, she had listened to the concept of noticing and not understood it. In fact, had felt mentally inadequate because she couldn't seem to grasp the idea. And all the time it really was a form of telepathy.

Grrr, thought Alpha.

She actually sat up, intending to have it out with Jane. And then, memory came. The real problem, momentarily pushed away, rolled back over her and into her. Down she sagged, back onto the bed. All right, she thought wearily, the prisoner could still get overwrought about French lessons on the eve of execution. I suppose if I believed in Karma, it would be a good indicator for my next life.

Her mother had recently taken up the Hindu past and future life idea. It was a pleasant prospect to contemplate, but Alpha would have none of it, particularly since Jane's grandmother had immediately started to talk about having an android duplicate made of her late husband. Alpha was vaguely ashamed of the implication of the older woman's intention, but she couldn't for the life of her see how such a down-to-earth purpose could derive from the, to her, unreal philosophy.

That afternoon –

As Alpha passed the kitchen door she heard Jane's voice say, 'You have to think what would happen to you, personally, if it didn't work –'

The woman stopped, and thought *Is that Jane One*

*or Jane Two*? She focused her mind on a dimly seen visualization of the android Jane after the manner the human Jane had described to her. She stared inwardly at the vague mental image, hoping to perceive in it something that would tell her which Jane's voice she had heard.

As usual, she drew a blank. With a sigh, she pushed the partly open door open another foot. Dan Two and Alpha Two stood with their backs to her. Beyond them, lying face down on the floor, was another android, someone she had never seen before.

Kneeling beside the stranger was Jane. She had a thin screwdriver and she was poking it gingerly in the rear of the prostrate one's right heel. She was saying, 'If you wish, I'll free you completely right now.'

'No, no,' came the muffled baritone voice, 'I'd better not do that until after your father comes. Just change what we discussed –'

The intent Alpha must have made a sound, for Dan Two and Alpha Two turned simultaneously.

'Excuse me,' said Alpha, 'I heard Jane's voice –'

Jane was rising. 'It's all right, Mother, I'm finished.'

Alpha suppressed her embarrassment at having been caught spying. 'What are you doing?' she asked.

It was Dan Two who answered. 'Your daughter,' he said, 'brought to our attention that if your husband comes tomorrow in an armed combo, it won't do any good to shoot at him.'

The words were so deadly that Alpha was suddenly breathless. When she could speak again, she said huskily, 'I thought he was to come over here so that somebody could talk to him.'

Dan Two said in a reassuring tone, 'Assassinating him was never really considered feasible, since Mr. Thaler is noted for his astuteness.'

The android, who had been lying on the floor,

climbed to his feet. He seemed to take it for granted that he had a right to participate in the conversation for he interjected, 'Jane pointed out that it won't do any good to fire at him because his combo will be equipped with those automatic bullet-dissolver-in-flight machines.'

Alpha had a memory. Something Dr. Camm had once said, 'Your daughter, Mrs. Thaler, is easily the best friend the androids on this planet ever had. She wants to free them all.'

Jane's voice came matter-of-factly. 'I explained that if Dad came in an armed combo, not only would it have the bullet-dissolver but it would also be equipped with small missiles that seek out rifles and energy weapons the instant they're discharged. And, of course, that's the end of whoever is holding the gun.

'So,' Jane continued, 'the watchers have been coming in and getting reprogrammed on that aspect.'

Alpha made a small, wordless sound, but dared not say anything coherent.

Jane was going on, 'My point was that whoever had programmed them didn't seem to care how dangerous it was for them.'

Dan Two added in a critical tone, 'The way this is going to be handled is, first, your husband will be dealt with, and then your daughter will program us to be completely free.'

Alpha flashed, 'Why don't you have Jane re-program you before my former husband shows up tomorrow?'

Dan Two gave her a startled look. 'But then I'd be free and wouldn't have to do what my programming now calls for.' He shook his head unnecessarily. 'That would be illogical.'

His genuine bewilderment alerted the woman. She said quickly. 'All you'd have to do is make up your mind in advance to carry through on the programming even if it isn't there.'

'But then I wouldn't have to do it.' He was clearly disturbed, for he repeated, '– Wouldn't have to.'

'You would if you decided you would,' the woman urged.

'No,' Dan Two shook his head for emphasis. His expression was suddenly stubborn. 'It wouldn't work,' he said.

Alpha gave up.

Jane accompanied her mother into her bedroom. She watched as Alpha dragged herself into the bed and then she spoke in a slightly critical voice, 'Mother, I hope you won't do that again.'

The woman stared blankly at the little girl in the pretty pink dress. She had the distinct feeling she was hearing nonsense words. Finally, 'Do what?'

'Interfere with my tests.' The girl wiggled her body impatiently. 'We don't really have that much time.'

'What tests?' said Alpha.

The girl did not reply immediately. Instead, she went over to a chair, sat down, and closed her eyes.

After a little, she said softly, 'I have an image of Dad, and I'm noticing a thought into it which says, "What you asked me to do, to persuade the androids to let me free them right away, won't work. They cannot go that much against their programming." When I persisted, and when Mother came in unexpectedly and tried to persuade them too, the androids became suspicious. I have a feeling the subject can't be brought up anymore. So what now?'

Over on the bed, Alpha whispered guiltily, 'Why didn't you warn me in advance?'

Over in the chair, Jane stirred and opened her eyes. Then she got up and came rapidly to the bed, leaned over Alpha and whispered, 'Dr. Camm will come some time this afternoon to evaluate the situation. We must act as if it's one of his occasional routine visits.'

Alpha whispered back, 'But what does he expect to accomplish?'

'I've told you everything that I noticed in Dad's image except, of course, that he was in a combo-cruiser flying over the city and I could feel that he's very determined, like he always *is*.'

The woman scarcely heard the final words. She was experiencing indignation. *Evaluation*, she thought scathingly. *We can evaluate it right here, for heaven's sake, as being absolutely –*

Her thought poised. She hadn't realized to what abyss it was taking her. All in a moment she was on the brink of the incredible reality. For just an instant, she cast a mental glance ahead at the madness that awaited them the following morning.

Alpha drew back, shuddering. She made an inner effort, then. To her great relief, the curtain came back down over her mind and there was all that lulled feeling again.

By that time, Jane was at the door of her bedroom. Over her shoulder, the girl said, 'See you at dinner, Mom.'

The interview ended like that, with the emotional equivalent of a dull plop. Alpha continued to lie there. Once the phone rang, but she had been warned against answering. She presumed that whoever was phoning was being suavely taken care of by one or other of the androids. Finally, there was a knock on her door, a pause, and then Dan Two came in.

'Dr. Camm is coming,' he said. 'We want you to stay in here.'

Alpha stirred in spite of herself. Amazingly, the earlier hope came back and she could feel color returning to her cheeks.

'We have no idea what he wants,' Dan Two went on, 'but your daughter says that he makes periodic visits like this.'

Alpha nodded her agreement, but she dared not speak.

'The way we're going to handle it,' said the android, 'is, your daughter and Alpha Two will go out shopping, and Jane Two will talk to the psychologist.'

No matter how many times Alpha ran her thought through that, she couldn't imagine how it could lead to a proper 'evaluation.' She realized presently that Dr. Camm had arrived, and after half an hour, when a distant door closed, that he had left. Came another knock, and once more Dan Two entered. 'He's gone,' he said. He stood there, lean, handsome, and discontented. 'That was an unusual coincidence,' he said, 'his showing up here today.'

'What happened?' Alpha's equally taut voice cut across the android's uneasiness. 'What did he want?'

The perfect duplicate of her ex-husband continued to frown. But he said, 'The questions he asked Jane Two – obviously believing he was talking to Jane One – seemed unimportant. School work? Relations with you and us. That's all.'

It was almost six o'clock when Jane One and Alpha Two returned home.

Jane was already at the dinner table when Alpha entered. The woman said, 'I'm your real mother, in case you're wondering.'

Her thought was simply to reassure Jane so that she could report freely on the afternoon's activities to her mother.

Jane gave her a momentarily baffled look, then shrugged and said, 'Who else would you be?'

'Alpha Two.'

'But she's in the kitchen,' Jane pointed out.

Alpha said no more. She had spent a griefy afternoon, and Jane was apparently choosing to ignore the fact that androids were now perfect duplicates. Alpha said wearily, 'If you're ever in doubt, don't hesitate to ask.'

'It's not one of my problems,' said Jane, with dignity.

All through dinner the girl seemed unusually cheerful. She spoke brightly to Dan Two when he brought the entree, called out compliments to Alpha Two in the kitchen on the tastiness of the food, and was generally very trying.

Her mood changed suddenly when Dan Two disappeared into the kitchen to get dessert. Then she said in a low voice, 'I was able to notice into the image of Alpha Two a feeling of nothing-wrong if I wandered away from her in the store. So she didn't worry when I went down an aisle and around a corner where Dad was waiting. He gave me a microphone, which I'm supposed to keep on me tomorrow morning.'

Alpha sat there and grappled with the tiny piece of information. She was normally full of confidence in her ex-husband and could, on occasion, even feel slightly amused by his reason for having divorced her the first year of their marriage – because she had followed her mother's advice and tried to handle him the way Mrs. Jonathan had controlled Alpha's father.

('Any daughter,' Dan had said when he originally departed, 'who could accept the advice of such a mother even for one minute, cannot be trusted as a wife.')

'A microphone!' she thought now. 'It will record whatever happens tomorrow morning and the result of that will, no doubt, be useful as evidence, if the case ever comes to trial.'

She realized she was fighting a strong tendency to be critical of Dan. He had actually had his own daughter out where he could have rescued her. But instead of whisking her to safety, he had allowed her to come back into a trap of unknown deadly potentiality. It seemed to her that no matter what the risk to the older people, surely the child should not be subjected to such stress.

As Alpha reached that point of internal protest, Jane glanced quickly at the kitchen and then whispered, 'So you see, Mom, that what Dad has done plus what I can do solves the whole problem.'

'Uh!' gaped Alpha. It was her most unladylike moment in many a long year.

Before she could pursue the matter, Dan Two came back in and, simultaneously, Jane stood up briskly. 'No dessert for me,' she said. She continued happily, 'I think I'll have Jane Two juice up on Sanskrit, and I'll talk with her for a while.'

The male android gazed after her as she went out. 'Where did she learn all those languages?' he asked. 'Jane Two tells me that your daughter has already talked five languages with her.'

'She's discovered a knack,' was all Alpha could trust herself to say.

'For a human being,' commented Dan Two tolerantly, 'she's pretty good. But,' he grew serious, 'there's something else more important I want to ask you.'

He sank into the chair across the table from Alpha. He regarded her soberly. He said, 'Is there a signal you give her?'

'How do you mean?' In surprise.

'She knows which is you without uncertainty.'

The woman gazed at the android uneasily. The question somehow threatened ... Jane. Threatened her, now. At once. Not later. Alpha thought tensely, 'If I say the truth, that there's no signal, will that be against Jane or for her?'

Before she could resolve the complexity, Dan Two seemed to come to a decision. And, in fact, a moment later he said, 'I'll ask Dr. Schneiter about it in the morning.'

The threat receded as rapidly as it had come. Alpha stood up and excused herself. The new thought was that she must ask Jane about the meeting in the store and the rationale of the optimistic conclusions about it.

Catching Jane turned out to be not simple at all. The first time she glanced into her daughter's bedroom, she saw an entrancing sight. The two Janes were sitting up on adjoining twin beds. As Alpha entered, both girls waggled their blonde tresses and gazed at her expectantly with duplicate pairs of blue eyes.

One of the duo said, 'We're doing an African dialect, Mother. It's really something.'

Alpha withdrew hastily, saying, 'See you later.'

But when she approached the door the next time, she could hear what sounded like ancient gypsy music playing. And when she peered in, the two girls were arrayed in blues and reds and dancing wildly, but gracefully.

That did it. As she walked away, Alpha thought *Really, it's much better for her to be doing diverting things than for me to ask her to explain exactly how she thinks this whole problem has been solved when, in fact, I may prove that it isn't.*

She spent the rest of the evening in the same peculiar quandary as she had the afternoon. She would lie down and then start to get up. Then would come the mental admonishment *Better lie down again.* *Conserve your strength.* And she would dutifully stretch out once more.

Somewhere in there, she slept.

Alpha woke up and had several almost simultaneous awarenesses.

Bright sunlight was pouring through her view window. Soft music was playing, she recognized one of her favorite classical works. Her bed-end clock showed 7:58 – 8/23/87. Alpha Two stood at the foot of her bed, beyond the clock. And one of the Janes, dressed for outdoors, along with Dan Two similarly arrayed, was standing in her doorway.

The girl said, 'I got up early, Mom, and Dan Two and I went down and watched Dr. Schneiter being released from jail.'

'It was the rational thing to do,' said Dan Two. 'That way, we established that he was actually released.'

The woman dared not speak right away. She swallowed, felt baffled, had the thought *Was this trip necessary?* and then managed, 'He was released?'

'At seven o'clock this morning,' said Jane cheerfully. 'Dan and I stood in the background, but I got a perfect image of him.'

The android corrected, 'She means she got a good look at him.'

'I guess that's what I mean,' said the girl. She waved. 'See you at breakfast, Mom.'

Whereupon, she and Dan walked off out of sight.

As the human woman brought her attention back to her own duplicate, the android who looked and acted like her said in a perfect imitation of Alpha's musical voice, 'Madam, we think you should get dressed. It's about to be eight o'clock and your husband is coming.'

Breakfast was served to her and Jane by two

102

nervous androids who kept glancing through the window toward the street. Abruptly, they must have seen what they were looking for. 'Here he comes!' The speaker was Alpha Two, and she was visibly upset. Her voice sounded semihysterical.

For a long moment that completely distracted the human woman from the information that the words conveyed, she thought *Do I sound like that, ever?*

Dan Two was speaking: 'We'll have to hide from him until Dr. Schneiter arrives,' he seemed to be pointing the explanation directly at Alpha, 'so you'll have to serve yourself.'

With that, the two androids hurried through the alcove that separated the breakfast room from the dining room. Next, they headed through the second alcove to the living room, and they separated. Alpha Two exited by way of the patio door and Dan Two disappeared through the door of the combination music room-library.

As he vanished, the phone rang.

'I'll take it in here,' Dan Two's voice came eerily floating out from his hiding place. He added, 'And when Dr. Thaler comes in, tell him to sit down and make no sudden moves. We've got you and your daughter covered.'

Alpha wasn't quite sure how he could both answer the phone and participate in keeping them 'covered.' But, in a way, she believed, and she had no intention of testing the claim.

In the distant room, there was a pause. Then Dan Two's voice, sounding somewhat more subdued but still audible, said 'Yes, Dr. Schneiter, everything is fine. He'll be entering in a minute, just in time for breakfast, so come over any time –'

At that point, Alpha happened to glance at Jane. She was startled to see that the girl was leaning back in her chair with her eyes closed.

'What? –' the woman began vaguely.

A finely shaped hand and arm waved her into silence. 'Ssshh,' admonished Jane, 'I'm noticing two things at the same time. It's hard.'

At least a minute went by, and then Jane opened her eyes. 'All right,' she said, 'that's done.'

The sun was shining through the dinette window. Out there was cloudless brightness, and the brilliance of it spilled across the finely netted table cloth and the gleaming dishes.

Inside Alpha's skin was the intense darkness of fear and anticipation of the crisis that, with the coming of her former husband, was now upon them. Her daughter's words penetrated the psychic blackness like a single ray of light in stygian night.

The woman stirred, as if a warmth had momentarily thawed all the frozen distances within her. She ceased the automatic movements of eating, blinked and said, 'What's done?'

'I've finally figured it all out,' Jane replied. 'To be like is not to be but to be able.'

Alpha gazed blankly at her daughter, and with each passing moment the words the girl had spoken seemed more meaningless. And yet, in another part of her brain, the meaning made an impression of impact size ... 'I have just heard,' decided Alpha, 'one of those deep, deep thoughts with which philosophers confuse all of us poor nitwits with I.Q.'s of a mere 140 or so.'

Her mind poised because ... the words had come from her fourteen-year-old daughter whom she had always considered smart but not a genius.

'I resemble,' continued Jane, 'leads to "I can", and not to "I am".' She waved her left hand vaguely. 'All these years of living with duplicate parents,' she said, 'finally made me realize –'

Alpha was staring at the girl, blinking several times as she tried to grasp the obscure meanings that were being offered her. Whatever it was obviously couldn't be explained by the word, 'finally.' It must have been a maturing process, the brain constantly completing an identification, sorting out real fathers and mothers from android substitutes.

With that clarification, words came, a basic question. 'But what do you do?' Alpha virtually breathed.

'I,' announced Jane triumphantly, 'speak Latin, French, and probably any language I choose. But I have to be with an android who speaks those languages in order to do it.'

'You mean you read their minds?'

Jane made an infinitely resigned negating gesture with her head. 'For heaven's sake, Mother, I was tested for ESP and I'm zero at that. Didn't you hear a single word I said?'

Alpha did a mental glance back over the dialogue and swallowed her continuing bafflement. What she wanted most desperately to ask was, 'But can you do anything that will help us in this awful situation?'

She didn't say it. Instead, she finally ventured lamely, 'What you get out of this is a new ability to learn?'

'Mother! Didn't you hear what I said? I haven't learned anything. At least, not yet. Maybe it will work out that way in the long run. But the method doesn't require it.'

'What,' asked Alpha, bracing herself, 'is the method?'

'It comes from noticing. I've described that to you before.'

As she spoke the words, and saw her mother's

expression, Jane One shook her head at the hopelessness of this attempt at communication. She realized, once again, that these explanations were a gosh-awful waste of time.

*We really are different, we children brought up with the look-alike android parents ...*

Since there were no visible differences between the living human and the duplicate android, from babyhood she had had to find a new way of telling the difference.

In the early grades, when you did most of your school work away from home, you came rushing into the house after school and there was mother – or was it? For a moment, then, you had to notice.

In the brain, the process of noticing differences is normally a single act of long ago. You saw in that first instant thousands of differences between one person and all others. In that initial observation you made your decision as to who this was.

Thereafter, on seeing that individual or thinking about him, it was this decision that you brought into the forefront of your mind, and reaffirmed.

With a look-alike android, you couldn't make a final decision. So you had to notice each time. Thousands of noticings presently evolved in Jane a permanent projective circuit. There had even been a period when she had fought a silent battle with hallucination ... she kept seeing androids and their human look-alikes even when they weren't around.

Actual projections – out there – with three-dimensional reality. So she had to notice that. Presently, by being aware of differences, she gained control over the projections.

She had noticed quite early that the projection of an android look-alike was quite, quite, quite different from the projection of a human being. You could see inside a projection and observe the inner person. After that, she had perfect awareness. She simply looked at the projections fleetingly, almost automatically, whenever she was in the presence of a real human or an android duplicate. *And knew.*

End of problem? Well, not completely. Jane became weary of explaining the details to her mother. 'It's just there,' she would say. 'It's noticing.'

'But what do you notice?'

'For Pete's sake, Mother, I keep trying to tell you –'

As she had so often in the past, Alpha said now, sadly, 'Yes, I suppose you have.'

Far more important, and what seemed unhappily all too clear, was that noticing, or at least the portion of it relating to languages, did not provide any way of defeating the super-androids. 'I suppose,' she thought wearily, 'I'll have to leave that up to Dan –'

As he got out of his combo-cruiser and approached his former wife's residence, Dan Thaler was stimulated, but not surprised, when what seemed to be a thought from his daughter came into his mind. It was a hasty message. 'Dad, Dan Two is talking to Dr. Schneiter. I think you ought to hear what's being said. I'll try to let it pass through me, because I'm also noticing the image of Dr. Schneiter himself –'

'All right,' the man acknowledged.

He was, he realized, not as calm as he had been in his time. So he couldn't help but observe that the tension surrounding his personal life was occurring on a perfect morning. The sky was blue. At every level, the silent combo-cruisers like his own were in motion, doing some normal, unthreatened business. He sensed the vast city around him, but did not, as was his custom, try to savor the contentment of being alive on an August day in the wonderful year of 2288 A.D.

He didn't feel quite that contented. At least, not yet.

He was inside the high fence, and moving past the swimming pool when the next set of thoughts came to him. It was what the android was saying.

*Good girl!* he thought.

'– No, we won't tie him until you get here ... Why not tie him at once? Well, sir, as you know, the procedure was never part of the programming so this morning, when we analyzed this entire situation, we decided to handle it rationally ... That makes you suspicious. I don't see why. Androids are perfectly capable of sound reasoning ... No, it was not suggested to me, and I have not been reprogrammed ... Yes, there was one visitor. Dr. Camm showed up yesterday for one of his routine interrogations. We handled it very skillfully. Sent the girl out with Alpha Two, and had him talk to Jane Two.'

There was a pause. The human Dan presumed that Dr. Schneiter, at the other end of the phone, was evaluating what had happened to his perfect trap.

Dan continued to move forward. But now he could give more attention to the familiar, two-level house in front of him. He actually felt well-protected by the automatic machinery in his combo, acting through instruments that he carried in his coat. But, nonetheless, he was glad when he saw no shadowy figure at any window, nor was there a movement on the roof or in the shrubbery at the side of the house. Glad, because you could never tell, these days, what new devices existed. He, who knew so many such things, respected the impossibility of any one person ever knowing everything that could be done against a living creature.

But he got safely to the stairs, and he started climbing.

Inside the house, the long silence was suddenly

broken. Dan Two called out, 'Alpha Two, were you separated from Jane in any way while you were out with her? Dr. Schneiter wants to know.'

As the android, Alpha, was yelling that information, the hall door opened, and the real Dan walked in. He came rapidly through the kitchen, into the breakfast room, and sat down. Alpha did a gesture thing with her arm, which was intended to be a welcome. Jane did not move, did not open her eyes, said nothing.

From where he sat, Dan could now also hear the voice of his duplicate, who said, 'I don't see how that would be a problem. If Alpha Two thought it was all right, then it was. After all, she's an android, with what that means in terms of superior ability to reason –'

As those words were spoken, Jane One opened her eyes and gave her father a quick smile. 'They really are awfully conceited,' she whispered.

Dan One whispered back, 'Somebody figured out that that was the way to program them, the idea being they couldn't be reasoned with by us. So we're taking full advantage of that.' He added, 'Of course, in order to do so we needed somebody who can put –' He stopped, and then finished – 'who can notice thoughts into images of other people and into androids.'

'Ssshh,' said Jane. Her eyes closed.

Dan Two's voice came, 'Yes, Jane Two is here. That's something we want to talk to you about. Whoever put that bomb into her was not thinking of what could happen to her ... No, that's been reprogrammed out. If the extreme act becomes necessary, she had Mrs. Thaler's gun ... The whole dilemma is right there. When we analyzed this situation, we discovered there was no clear-cut moment for Jane Two to shoot. So she will remain in hiding until you come over here and have your conversation with Mr. Thaler. And if you don't come, we'll set the whole thing up again for tomorrow morning. And so on . . . Yes, I heard him come in. I'll ask him if he's willing to talk to you.'

He called, 'Dan One, would you pick up the phone in the breakfast room? Dr. Schneiter would like to talk to you.'

Dan said, 'It must be understood that my talking to him now will in no way be construed as being the conversation which Doctor Schneiter originally intended to have with me here.'

After Dan Two had communicated that into the phone, he called, 'It is understood.'

Smiling faintly, the man, whose presence was already making Alpha feel better, reached to the little table by the window and picked up the receiver. 'Hello,' he said, 'that was a pretty rational account, don't you think?'

'High praise, indeed,' said Dan Two's voice out of the receiver, 'coming from someone like you. I'll hang up now, gentlemen.' There was a click.

Dan said, 'Well, Doctor, I gather you're not going to show up here as you were originally scheduled to do.'

The familiar voice at the other end sounded resigned. 'Mr. Thaler, we seemed to have arrived at an impasse.'

Dan urged, 'You have an edge, since you're no longer in jail.'

'I don't know exactly what you did,' sighed the older man, 'but as I see it, the situation is a permanent trap for all of us.'

In a few sentences, he thereupon listed the binding elements of their condition. The androids would always hide when Dan was in the house. And one or other would always accompany Alpha or Jane, but would not allow them to go out together. They would only tie up Dan if Schneiter actually entered the house. Which, of course, it would be ridiculous for him to do in view of the weapons that Dr. Camm had undoubtedly brought into the house on his 'routine' call, plus whatever Jane had brought back from the store.

'The situation is even more binding than that,' said Dan. 'They considered all the possibilities as they might apply in future. They will let me leave at 10:30 every morning, but insist I come back next morning by 8, in case that's the morning you decide to come over. They recognize that this might be inconvenient for me, so they are agreeable to my coming here the night before and remaining all night. But, since it would be an immoral thing for me to stay with my ex-wife, they insist that we remarry.'

There was silence at the other end. When the older man's voice came again, there was in his tone that cheerfulness which some males feel when another has got himself into a severe female predicament.

'Well, well,' he said, 'I'm beginning to make my peace with what has happened. I can't see a married Dan Thaler being as dangerous to my plans as a single one has been. And you will be in that perpetual trap, won't you?'

He finished almost happily, 'I'll call from time to time to make sure that nothing has changed.'

There was a click of disconnection.

Jane could have pointed out to the two men that there were several additional consequences. The androids were now forever in a position where they could have their freedom; but, of course, they couldn't accept. And, therefore, they had to stay, and stay. And, besides –

'The situation,' she explained, 'is really much better than he said, because I noticed into the image of Dr. Schneiter that all this using of androids wasn't really worth going to jail for.'

To her mother, she said, 'It's rather interesting that this method I have of controlling adults by noticing thoughts into their images doesn't seem to bother my conscience anymore, once I realized that that was the only way I could get a sister.'

The adults stared at her, but said nothing. Jane said 'Right now, Mother is wondering if we've got a little monster on our hands, but she's not really disturbed – yet. And Dad is thinking in that determined way of his that even you, Mom, are going to have to learn to notice when somebody is putting a thought about going to sleep into your image, like I did yesterday so you wouldn't worry. He's also thinking that training a hundred thousand like me is going to take fourteen years, but right now I'm all he's got against whoever is using the androids to take over the world.

'He's wondering if I'll even things up in that fight. Well,' she slipped off her chair, 'I think I'll go and learn another language, or another dance, or another science, or another, or another –

'And if I do all of those things in time, Dad, maybe I will.'

# THE FIRST RULL

As HE saw the photographic plate, the Rull, who reflected the human appearance of a man called Zebner whom he had killed, found himself in a losing battle with an impulse.

No, you've got more important things to do. A bigger fish to catch.

His thought was actually that colloquial, a product of his enormous effort since his arrival on earth to project not only the dead Zebner's body image but also his verbal and mental mannerisms.

Outwardly, the Zebner body made no apparent move; did not turn, seemed not to be concerned if anyone else was around. But, in fact, the Rull perceptive system made a lightning survey of the big university laboratory, peering with more than just ordinary intensity and awareness through the energy screen from behind which he operated with a tireless vigilance. What he saw seemed incredible. Emptiness. Not a soul in sight. Hard to accept, but after a moment he realized why.

– This is Saturday afternoon. Nobody here but us saboteurs . . . One saboteur only, of course. Himself.

Again, poised there, the Rull argued against his desire to take advantage of his accidental noticing of the photographic plate. He realized fully what a fantastic, neglectful thing somebody had done. He recognized the plate as one of a recent series brought back from a distant space experiment costing in the millions, which he could nullify totally by simply appearing to put out one human hand –

He manipulated the human image so that the hand and arm seemed to reach out.

– Picking up the plate.

A Rull feeler grasped the plate, though the human hand appeared to be doing the lifting and holding. And dropping it forcefully into the empty, metal wastepaper basket, and applying energy.

It dropped, propelled by a hard shove from the feeler.

The crash, as the negative shattered into dozens of pieces, was like a signal. A girl entered the door farthest away and started along one of the aisles heading in the general direction of the Rull spy.

Furious, the Rull swerved and walked rapidly off toward an opposite door. As he hurried down a back stairs, then outside, then close to a wall, then other roundabouts, his human face reflected nothing of the self-reproach he was experiencing. On the face was a smile.

But the thought was *Unwise. A foolish action. Now, there would have to be cover-up acts. And alibis, most likely.*

Still thinking thus a few minutes later, he knocked at the door of Peter Gilstrap. The small man who answered the knock hesitated as he saw who it was, then reluctantly stepped aside. The creature entered, giving Zebner's heartiest hello, and sat down beside a desk that had textbooks and notebooks spread out on it.

Carefully imitating Zebner's somewhat harsh voice, he explained that he had not recently noticed Gilstrap, and was everything all right? As he completed the question, it occurred to the Rull that the words had an unfortunate connotation. There was an implication that he was seeing Gilstrap for the first time in a long period. A wrong admission.

Mentally, he retraced his words. He analyzed that his approach should have been more casual. No mention of time. Perhaps even assume that they had daily contact ... The Rull emerged from his self-absorption with the awareness that Gilstrap had said something, and he had no idea what.

Act as if he had, of course. Move verbally forward, past the human being's remark. 'How's the homework coming?' The Zebner imitation voice boomed in the small room. The image of Zebner's hand motioned at the desk, where the books were.

The reply to that should have been, and was, ordinary enough. Gilstrap was getting along all right in everything except physics. Dr. Lowery was a difficult teacher; fortunately, not impossibly so.

They had discussed the subject before, and the Rull had always been careful not to reveal his growing hatred of the physics professor. Rull science was in every way superior to human, and yet a master of that science was on the verge of being flunked by an Earth college teacher.

The recollection seemed to take its mind off into a

117

corner – for moments only. Yet, when he came to awareness, it was to the sound of the Zebner voice raging, 'That stupid fool. The science of physics is a thousand years old, but finally there comes Herman Lowery, the teacher who alone knows how it should be. And nothing else will do but that we must learn it with his special imprint. The way of atoms and molecule complexes –' he finished scathingly, 'strained through his sickly, egotistical brain.'

He stopped the ranting because there was an expression of surprise on Gilstrap's somewhat heavy countenance. The Rull forced the smile back on Zebner's face. Before he could apologize, the little man said, 'What other way is there to teach physics?'

Nothing, of course, to say to that. He should never have allowed his emotion to show. These students were experiencing physics for the first time. They couldn't make a comparison as could a Rull science master.

Again, an error. Striving for recovery, the Rull glanced at the image of a human-made wrist watch, consulted his own inner time sense in relation to Earth, made the Zebner face frown and the Zebner voice say, 'Oh, my gosh, it's nearly three –'

It was actually after three. But if he could put over that he had been here . . . earlier . . . during the event in the lab –

He was on his feet. As he strode – that was the appearance – to the door, he called over his shoulder loudly, 'Great to see you, old man. Glad all is well. But it's back to homework for both of us. Dr. Lowery is a fierce tyrant of the classroom, as you may have guessed from my loud and painful squealing.'

Outside, still reacting to his unanticipated outburst of rage, the Rull headed down the street to his own quarters. He laid the powerful wormlike body on the bed, put the Zebner image into the appearance of sleep, and considered the problem he had created for himself.

Final decision: since it was still weekend, he could very likely sneak back into the lab, carry the wastebasket to a trash receptacle and thus dispose of the shattered photographic plate before anyone found it and discovered that the tough material had been subjected to a specific energy flow.

Solution not too satisfactory. But, still, it was weekend, that period of time when all student life flowed past the classrooms instead of into them. In fact, one of the difficulties was that he might be one of only a few in the gigantic network of corridors and buildings.

It was a chance that would have to be taken. Tomorrow, Sunday ... Having made the decision, he got up and forced himself to sit down to do his homework. He did it carefully, trying to remember the exact format of presentation required by that mad genius, Dr. Lowery. For a time – a dangerously long time – he had resisted the method until he had aroused in the older (than Zebner) man's paranoid instructional brain the antagonism that had now twice earned him a D-minus.

... Really ridiculous. Naturally, the Rull high command had sent a very special science master on this first exploratory trip to Earth.

Sunday came. The Zebner image entered the laboratory door which was partly open. He went boldly into the museum-like unoccupied vastness straight to the wastebasket, bent over it to pick it up, and saw that the basket was empty.

Dismay. Momentarily came the wonder *Wrong basket*? The Rull calmed his inner disturbance while he hastily measured distances and sized up his surroundings. On such details his perceptive system was infallible. This was the one. Unquestionably.

He made his way unseen back to his room and he was, he told himself, pleased. To have gone and looked was right.

Two possibilities, it seemed to the Rull, existed for the disappearance of the plate. The girl who had entered Saturday had seen, at a distance, somebody demolish it, and had rescued the destroyed object and transported it to some unknown receptacle. Or else the university maintenance department had, in the course of routine disposition of the contents of wastebaskets, disposed of those fragments, also.

Both possibilities had encouraging elements for a saboteur. If it was the girl, she had not recognized Zebner, else the police would already have been to his rooms. The other possibility, the emptying of the basket by the men in white, offered no problems at all.

During the rest of Sunday afternoon and evening, the alien being allowed himself an occasional moment of relaxed mind and body as these reassurances repeated in his mind. The good feeling collapsed during the first Monday class, when the English instructor handed him a sealed letter, which, when opened, revealed a note from Dr. Lowery requesting 'Mr. Zebner' to report to the doctor's private office during his lunch hour.

That had never happened before.

As he entered the office, the Rull saw the angular, seated Dr. Lowery, and beyond him, seeming quite nervous, a pretty senior student named Eileen Davis. She was a girl who was in two of Zebner's classes, and she had, in the past, always avoided him.

During his initial investigation into the backgrounds of all of the class members of his various classes, he had discovered that she belonged to a student commune. Moreover, on instructions of her commune leader, she occasionally – about once a month – slept with Professor Lowery. Also, she had other sexual activities going forward on a regular basis.

It was actually a lucky activity for her. Because the Zebner-Rull had toyed with the possibility of duplicating the image of one of the young women, and his first impulse, when he detected her instant dislike of him, had been to duplicate her ... Impossible, of course, the moment he realized how many intimate associations the girl had.

Eileen did not really care for the duty stint with the physics professor, but it was part of the commune's con on behalf of those of its members who were in Lowery's class. She was the good guy who got everybody good grades. On that basis, she was glad to do the job that no other girl wanted. But her face was now pale, and she was gazing steadily off to one side.

The gangling professor, with the streaks of raw, purple-red color in his cheeks, must have motioned Zebner into a chair on the opposite side of the desk, because that was where he was suddenly sitting. From that unhappy position, he was able to observe Dr. Lowery and to realize that all was not well.

The older man was in a severe state. His lower lip trembled. When he picked up a pen, which he did for a doodling, not a rational, reason, his fingers couldn't seem to grasp it firmly. He held the pen awkwardly, as a small child might.

*Strong, regressive tendencies*, thought the Rull.

Instantly, he felt a strain. He had, by now, seen several people who had had their defenses broken down. And all his experiences with such persons had been unpleasant.

With a visible grimace, the older man seemed to

recover. 'Mr. Zebner,' he began, 'a valuable photographic plate was destroyed in the laboratory on Saturday, and Miss Davis says that she saw you destroy it. That is a very serious offense, and I am going to be compelled to call the authorities unless you can quickly explain the circumstances of the destruction.'

It was attack, the direct approach. Typical of the stubborn, stupid fellow. In fact, it was so direct that the Rull, though he had been bracing himself all morning, flinched.

Nevertheless, after a moment he managed to say his prepared first reaction, 'What did you say I did?'

Lowery repeated his accusation ... and Eileen Davis changed the direction of her stare. Some of the white of her cheeks yielded to a touch of color. Abruptly, she seemed doubtful.

The Rull noticed, and said firmly, 'But, sir, I was not in this building on Saturday.'

'Miss Davis says she saw you.'

'That's impossible,' Zebner's voice was positive. 'I'm sure I can prove that I was somewhere, though right off I don't recall all my movements.' He frowned. 'When was this?'

Thus, the dialogue proceeded along the channels that he had laid down for himself.

Just where Miss Davis interrupted, the Rull was not afterwards quite clear. But she made a sound. It was a sound without direct meaning. Inarticulate. Yet somehow it was a statement.

The Rull had been observing the girl with his wide-range perception. At this moment, an amazing complex of energy waves emitted from her. Seen on the level of Zebner's limited vision, her face was brick red. But at the other levels came an additional message: she was showing awareness of her dislike of

Zebner. And she was thinking – a whole band of infrared frequencies showed it – that she had allowed personal animosity to lead her to a positive identification in an area where she had merely jumped to a conclusion.

The fact that her identification of Zebner in that single, distant glance, was correct was no help to her in this moment of her agonizing doubt.

As these side reactions occurred, the Rull arrived verbally at the point where, suddenly, he considered it convenient to remember where he had been Saturday afternoon:

'Oh, yes, I dropped in and chatted with my fellow student, Gilstrap, who lives down the street from me. Now, I remember –'

After these words, there was little more to say. Dr. Lowery formally dismissed Zebner, murmuring something about checking into the matter further.

As the Rull walked out the door, the girl was still sitting in the chair beside the professor's desk. Since he would see them both in his last class of the day, the physics class, the alien did not linger. With his insides like stinging jelly, he flowed toward his first afternoon class.

What bothered the Rull as he retreated was that he should have known. The professor had, by his colossal need to subordinate physics to his own ego and make it a sort of sub-branch of the super-science of Lowery-ology, had, by that continuous madness, actually made visible the severity of his mental state to anyone who could detect such things.

*And I let his conceit hurt my feelings* ... He had taken it for granted that he would be an A-student, somehow recognized by the instructor as a peer – *you stupid fool!* The Rull raged at himself.

During Lowery's class, the Rull studiously avoided

the glances Eileen sent in Zebner's direction. But he had his own intuition that her tattling on Zebner had achieved for him and her a relationship – temporary, yes, but definite.

So, as the class adjourned, he intercepted her and asked her in a low voice, a neutral, non-antagonistic tone, 'What happened after I left?'

She gave him her first warmth, a direct look which had in it gratitude that he was not angry, an anxiety to communicate conciliatory information. 'I told him I must have been mistaken,' she said.

Having thus wiped away her sin, she brightened and said in a friendly voice, 'Dan would like to know if you'd care to join our group?'

The Rull happened to know that Dan was the leader of her commune, and so this was a victory of sorts of which, of course, he could not take immediate advantage. Later, he thought, the intimacy that is being offered will give me an opportunity to consume this girl. But at the moment, her offer seemed like another way to confuse Professor Lowery, so his outward response was a Zebner smile, instant acceptance, and the words, 'Can you come to my rooms tonight and get acquainted?'

The girl's color was high. It was clearly hard for her to accept Zebner even in a love-everybody commune situation. But she said, 'What time?'

'Oh, about 10 o'clock.'

She arrived on time, and she had evidently braced herself. She was bright, cheerful, smiling. Her black hair gleamed. She said, 'You stay here, and I'll call you!' and she marched straight into his bedroom and closed the door.

It took awhile, but presently her voice came with a lilting sweetness in it. When the disguised Rull entered, there she was in his bed, with a thin sheet pulled up as far as her waist. Her nude body was tanned, and so far as the alien could make out, was a good example of human female pulchritude. 'I've got a lot of homework still to do tonight. So let's get this first time over with. Okay?'

The Rull sat down across the room from her and had the Zebner face smile at her. 'I just thought we'd get acquainted tonight,' the Zebner voice said.

It actually took several minutes to convince the unbelieving girl. Finally, swallowing, she said, 'Can I use your phone? I want to call my commune leader.'

She talked briefly to 'Dan' and then laid the instrument down on the bed. 'Dan wants to talk to you,' she said. As the Rull came over, she slipped out of the far side of the bed and began to get dressed.

Dan's voice was a soft baritone. He said, 'Zeb, I told Eileen to include you in her harem, and she agreed. So what's the problem?'

The Rull was at ease and instantly responded to the intimacy of tone. 'Look, Dan,' he said, 'this girl doesn't like me. So I'd rather take a little extra time, not rush her, and get her over this feeling that I'm a – whatever. And maybe, presently, get a real response from her.'

There was silence at the other end when those words had been spoken. Then a slow whistle. Finally, 'Okay, Zeb, put her back on.'

The conversation between Dan and Eileen was brief. They seemed to agree that it was an odd reaction, but not wrong.

Zebner went downstairs with her and walked her to her car. When she had driven off, he went across the street to another car. At his approach, Dr. Lowery raised himself up from the flat position to which he had ducked when Eileen and Zebner emerged. The expression on his face, as seen in the half-light, was not easy to evaluate.

Nevertheless, the Rull repeated the brilliant idea that had provided such a perfect explanation for Eileen Davis's naming him as the destroyer of the photographic plate, and which had motivated him to phone Dr. Lowery as soon as he realized the girl was actually going to come over to his apartment.

'– And to think,' he concluded, 'that I thought my little sweetheart was too naive for me. Immediately on my rejecting her, she goes to you and makes this wild accusation. So I thought I'd better win her back as you saw, until I find out what's going on.'

'And what did she tell you?' asked Dr. Lowery.

'Alas, womanlike, she refused to discuss the matter. I dared not press her this first after-time. So may I ask a question?'

If Dr. Lowery indicated yes or no, the Rull did not hear it or see it, so he rushed on without waiting, 'What is the history of that photo plate being in that lab and not in its proper protective vault?'

The dim figure in the car seemed to stiffen. From the darkness of the car, Dr. Lowery said in a formal tone, 'All information about a classified matter is itself classified, Mister Zebner.'

'But,' Zebner protested anxiously, 'since I've been accused, I should be allowed some clue –'

He was cut off. 'For an intimate friend,' said the older man scathingly, 'Miss Davis doesn't seem to have communicated very intimately with you.'

'You mean, she knows something? –'

The Zebner-Rull stopped because he had detected an odd note in Dr. Lowery's voice. Jealous, he thought. I'll be damned. He would have liked to have been in that bed tonight with Eileen . . . He swallowed a deep breath, then said in his best sly voice, 'Now, sir, as one man to another, you must know from your own marital and extra-marital associations that a woman will never admit anything that puts her in the wrong.'

Dr. Lowery was silent. He sat for a long moment in the shadowy depths of his car there under the tree, and then he leaned forward. The Ishmael engine, with its systematic opposites – molecule against molecule – purred. The machine leaped against the brake.

The Rull was suddenly frantic. He had the despairing feeling that he had not achieved the final ending of the affair that he had hoped for. He yelled, 'Is there anything more I can do, any help I can give?'

The motor was roaring, a shuddering sound – the brake was still on. Above that roar he thought he heard the words, 'We'll check further into your story and then call you –'

With a lurch, the automobile surged forward, breaking Zebner's hold on the front door. Helpless, he watched the entire configuration of moving vehicle, with its headlights probing the night street and its rear lights receding.

Silently, he cursed his impulse to destroy a mere multi million dollar program. By doing so, he had jeopardized his mission to this planet, the final act of which was intended to be the recovery of a lost Rull space vehicle.

The Zebner-Rull arose at six next morning. He had remembered what Dr. Lowery had said the previous night, 'Check further!' And he was realizing that the only place they could check was Gilstrap.

Seen in retrospect, his attempt to achieve an alibi looked more blatant than it had appeared to be at the time. More obviously a scheme. At the time, of course, he had simply tried to make it appear that he was casually stopping in at Gilstrap's quarters.

He had actually cultivated Gilstrap for some such

purpose, but he had not had enough spare moments to cultivate him properly. Instead, Dr. Lowery's study requirements had kept him in his own room, hard at work into the wee hours translating the truth of science into the twisted presentation method that Lowery's distorted ego had devised for his students.

With a grimace of Zebner's heavy face, he shifted his mind away from the instant rage that surged. Again he realized, it was a dangerous alibi, and perhaps the only thing that remained against him.

Unfortunately, there was not time to plan a subtle accident. The act of killing had to be tough and direct, and before they checked Gilstrap's story.

In a way, of course, it was not a severe problem. A dozen human beings had already died in this exploratory mission to Earth. The dead included the original Zebner, whom he had simply eaten, bones and all. Rulls had a high metabolism and were hungry almost all the time. Thus, he had disposed of Zebner in four days, and later he gobbled several other victims in the same way. But there was no time for that today. And, besides, he had become dutifully cautious and now ate beef and other purchasable items.

As he waited for Gilstrap, the scene was pleasantly anonymous at the campus level. An uncountable number of students had, minutes before, emerged from their classrooms. They were now walking, jogging, running, hurrying to what, for each individual, was undoubtedly a destination. But the details of that goal for each were available in the minds of a small number of persons – the student himself, and a few classmates, and was available also in administrative files. Nowhere else.

Report said that accepted registration totaled over 24,000, and that was a comfortable figure to contemplate. The largeness of the number was like a concealment of a special type. It equated with a dark night where, unseen, unnoticed assailants could attack without fear of being observed or afterwards recognized.

*There's Gilstrap!*

The little man emerged from the corridor exactly on schedule. His class ended, he was heading with 24,000 others to some logical place.

'Hi, there, Gil.' Zebner spoke heartily. 'May I have a word with you?'

He didn't wait for permission, but fell in step with the little guy and, as the other hesitated, caught his arm and said, 'Just thirty seconds!' Whereupon, Gilstrap relaxed and allowed himself to be guided into the selected death area.

'This way,' said the Rull triumphantly.

The victim was so unsuspecting that he even permitted himself to be turned away from the gun, which was now discharged into his left side.

The explosion was, of course, like the thunder of all guns. But Zebner trusted to the darkness of numbers, and, as Gilstrap staggered and fell, he swerved back the way he had come.

As he came swiftly to the entrance, a figure of a man loomed up in front of him. It was a young man. He stood there just inside the otherwise deserted alcove. His face was distorted with shock. His eyes were wide and staring.

'Hey!' he blurted, 'that was murder. What? –'

The Rull darted past him, whirled into a door, ran along a corridor past several students who did not even glance at him, out of another door, across a patio, down some steps, another patio, up some steps, into a second door, across to a distant exit, and there, breathing hard, he slowed, emerging at a walk in time to go into his next class.

After he had sat down in his careful fashion – it had to be careful because, of course, he actually had to get the Rull body into the seat while maintaining Zebner's image – he tried to recall what the witness had looked like. When he couldn't, he felt reassured.

Near the end of the third period, a messenger came to the door and handed a note to the instructor who, as the class ended, discreetly slipped it to Zebner. The shock of seeing the white envelope was relieved only by the Rull's argument to himself that it couldn't be anything important.

*If they're after me, really, they'll come with guns* he told himself. And thus calmed after leaving the room, he examined the envelope.

It had the words, *Administrative Office*, printed on the back flaps. That was shaking. And when he manipulated it open, the little note inside requested that he report to a Mr. Andrew Josephs during the lunch hour.

Mr. Josephs turned out to be a man with stiff body and grave manner. The Rull could not recall ever having seen him before, so he was relieved and courteously introduced himself, then waited with an outward air of equally courteous interest.

The big man stroked his jaw. 'I have two or three important pieces of news for you, Mr. Zebner. One of them is very sad. You may be interested to know that Miss Eileen Davis has definitely withdrawn her accusation against you. She is now convinced that you are not the person she saw.'

The Rull had the feeling that if the Zebner image so much as moved a muscle, the spell would be broken and he would find himself back in a world where people didn't alter their stories; where they did remember the truth, and told it fearlessly.

Mr. Josephs was continuing, 'Also, this morning we questioned your friend, Gilstrap and, of course, he verified your story of having been to his quarters on Saturday before three o'clock which, of course, is the decisive time.'

'He did?' said the Rull. But he said it deep inside the Zebner image field.

'Now, comes the sad part,' the man went on. 'This morning, after his first class, I have to tell you, this friend of yours was assassinated.'

It was evidently a very disturbing thing for him to report for he took out a large white handkerchief and blew his nose. Then he said, earnestly, 'Mr. Zebner, somebody has tried very hard to pin this unpleasant matter on you. And, of course, the police will now make a full investigation. But I want to assure you that we all exceedingly regret the inconveniences this has caused you.'

Whereupon, he held out his hand.

Naturally, the Rull pretended not to see it. After all, the untouchability of the original Zebner, the almost outcast status, was what had made the man his chosen victim. Close contact he dared not have, so he said, 'I'd better eat, sir, and get ready for my next class.'

'Yes, yes,' agreed Mr. Josephs, lowering his outstretched hand. He went on, 'We're baffled by the motive for these crimes, Mr. Zebner. What is puzzling us is that no secret work is being done at this college.' He concluded, 'When the police are ready, you will be called –'

The Rull went out into the corridor with those words echoing unhappily inside him. No question. He'd have to wind up his mission without having completed his study of human beings. It was time to make major decisions.

Along with several other Rulls, he had been sent to

Earth for two reasons. One, who are these two-legged beings that we Rulls have suddenly become aware of as we encroached on this new area of space? And, more important, what is the state of their technology? Purpose Two was the result of an unfortunate accident. On a remote solar meteorite, a human exploratory scientific group had found a lost Rull antigravity raft. Men still didn't know what a treasure they had. Fortunately, its damaged control box had been triggered when it was moved into the Earth spaceship. The fantastic machine had, of course, automatically transmitted a signal to its remote mother ship, reporting its position. Stunned Rull engineers traced its movements as it was taken to Earth.

The raft had been assigned to this university's physics department for research purposes, so the Rull had discovered, and a Professor Dr. Herman Lowery had succeeded in having the research on it assigned to him during his next vacation period, now slightly less than two months away.

Thus, after a careful survey of the physics department students, the Rull agent had chosen to imitate Zebner, a lackluster individual without friends.

Alas, Zebner was now a marked person.

The Rull skipped his afternoon classes and left the campus. Shortly before dusk, he headed for a designated rendezvous. At a certain hour every day, one of his Rull colleagues was supposed to come there in case of need.

The second Rull arrived on schedule, displaying the image of a very plain, unkempt human being; exactly the type of person that people would normally avoid. The two Rulls talked in their human voices, and the Zebner-Rull's decision was affirmed.

Tonight – act!

The Zebner-Rull thereupon returned to his apartment to get the equipment he had stored in his bedroom clothes closet for the time of destruction. He was intent. He was thinking about how he would transport it down to the garage, and so he was not wary. As he opened the door to the flat he sensed, for the first time, another presence in the interior. Instant attempt to pull back. Too late.

The voice of Professor Lowery said, 'I've got you covered. Get in here!'

Reluctantly, the Zebner image moved through the door and inside. His tentative plan was *Maybe as soon as I get across the threshold, I can move sideways into the blackness at Rull speed.*

'Careful!' came the inexorable voice. 'Reach over slowly and push the light switch.'

No choice. He deduced he was being watched through night-vision glasses.

The light revealed a Dr. Lowery with the night-vision glasses, watery eyes behind them, and a tormented face.

The instructor's heat-prod urged the Rull over to the breakfast nook. When he arrived there, the older man's hand indicated a paper that lay on the table. 'That,' he said harshly, 'is a confession. Sign it!'

Zebner was genuinely curious. 'What am I confessing to?'

'The truth. Sign it!'

*Not so fast* thought the Rull. *At this moment you need my signature* ... Until he inscribed his name, he could count on that fact to exercise a small restraint on Lowery's trigger finger.

While he considered what he should do with Lowery, and without waiting for permission, he moved over, bent over, and read the paper:

133

I, Phillip Zebner, having made up my mind to commit suicide, wish to rectify the harm I have caused. My most severe guilt concerns a very able person, my physics professor, Dr. Herman Lowery. Because of an emotional involvement with another student, Eileen Davis, and after a quarrel with her, I destroyed a certain photographic plate knowing it had been given into her care by Dr. Lowery –

At that point, having absorbed the import of the thing, the Rull said, 'Tell me why you entrusted Miss Davis with the photo plate.'

'I didn't know –,' mumblingly, 'that the person she wanted it for was one of her boy friends. I agreed he could do his B.A. thesis on the set. The fool carelessly laid one of the plates on another table off to one side. And so, when Eileen brought them back to me, that one was missing. That's when she returned to get it. I thought –' Lowery stopped, a sudden vagueness in his manner.

The Rull correctly interpreted that the unfinished sentence was not related to the explanation. 'You thought she was only fornicating with you?'

'Yes,' sighed the older man. He seemed bewildered.

The Rull asked quickly, 'How many people do you have to pass to have her?'

'When she finally admitted her situation to me,' Lowery sighed, 'it turned out that her commune leader, Dan, is so busy with his commune duties – I'm giving him an A.' He broke off, bitterly. 'They didn't take the breaking of the photo plate seriously.'

*That's it!* thought Zebner. He'd been listening every instant for something to grab onto and twist to his own purposes. 'Listen,' his human voice box spoke the thought, 'I'll admit that Eileen was my girl friend, but that she destroyed the plate –' He rushed on, 'The commune will assign you another one of their whores, but she's got to take the blame. I'll leave immediately and go back where I came from, and you send me an A rating there.'

'You'll get an A, don't worry. You're actually a good student, Zebner.'

*Now, he tells me!*

'Get me a sheet of paper from my work desk over there!' the Rull commanded.

Professor Lowery got the paper.

'Now, stand back!' That was because even in his overheated state, Lowery might notice how peculiarly Zebner wrote.

The confession, when completed, was as he had outlined it to Lowery but, of course, contained no suicide clause.

A considerably unglued, but grateful, Dr. Lowery accepted it and staggered out of the apartment. Zebner waited only until the man had had time to leave the building, then he boldly carried his equipment down the back elevator and into his car. He met no one, and he was relieved when he had driven safely out onto the street and was on his way, intending never to return.

Still later, when darkness had already settled over the great campus and enormous hivelike patterns of light brightened every building, the Rull drove into the parking lot of the research center. His companion was waiting for him there.

Darkness was probing everywhere when the two Rulls waylaid the stocky, baldheaded man who drove into the lot a few minutes later. They were remorselessly bold, killing him with energy flows from their own true bodies. There were bright flashes of light in that far corner of the lot where the guard

135

had put his car and apparently no one saw. It would have made no difference. On this night they were prepared to kill all witnesses.

Hurriedly, the two aliens stuffed the dead body into the trunk of the guard's own car, and then the second Rull did his image duplication of the man. He walked into the lobby and took over from the man on the previous shift. That individual departed at once.

There was now a quick examination of the sign-in book. It turned out there were eight people in the building. They locked the outer doors, then went from room to room and killed all eight with body energy discharges.

Still operating at top speed, the two experts brought in Zebner's destruct equipment and set it up where it would ignite the building best.

First, of course, they examined the disabled Rull anti-gravity raft. As expected, the problem was minor. The computer which, during power-on, reeducated the atoms, had decided that it required maintenance and had shut itself off. It turned on again immediately, on manual control, and was then good for many hours of trans-light operation. Enough.

In his physics class, the Rull had discovered that Earth science was just beginning to be aware that there were ways of modifying the behavior of particles. Earth had an anti-gravity technique based on simple, colossal power. It was not a system to be despised. By its means, great ships could lift routinely from the surfaces of ordinary planets, and with additional power unit attachments, could also depart heavier planets.

It was pretty good, but not in the same class as the Rull method. Long ago it had been discovered that atoms could be 'persuaded' to 'believe' that nearby masses (like a planet) did not exist. Accordingly, it and its fellow 'student' atoms were trained to ignore large bodies in space at the push of a button, to whatever degree was desired.

With the two Rulls aboard, the anti-gravity 'raft' floated up from the roof of the research center into the night sky. As soon as they were at a safe distance, the Zebner-Rull triggered the destruct system down inside the building, waited the exact number of seconds, and –

Nothing happened!

'That girl,' he analyzed finally, 'when she went into my bedroom to undress yesterday...' He should have realized when it took her so long. She must have searched the place, and, being a physics student herself, realized what was in the closet and removed the interior connectors.

He explained to his companion, 'I'll go back to my apartment and phone her to come over. Act as if I'm ready to have my affair with her. We'll take her along and eat her.'

It was important. There should be no clear evidence that the raft was missing. A fiery inferno would leave hundreds of metal hulks, sufficient to confuse a search for missing objects. And the girl's body, with the two already aboard ... food!

Down they went, onto the roof of his apartment building. From that roof, the Zebner-Rull made his way down a dark staircase to the upper inhabited level, and then down to his own apartment.

*First*, he thought, *I'll search the clothes closet* ... Hard to believe that he could have been so careless as to leave anything behind. But, still, check that. And then phone Eileen.

As he opened the door a minute later, pushed it wide and entered, at the final split-instant he had the horrifying realization that he had done it again. Impossible, but true! A Rull caught twice by the same situation.

At the moment of opening the door, the apartment was pitch dark. Then, as he stepped across the threshold, all the lights went on.

Now, when it was too late, his perception was swift. But it succeeded only in establishing at high speed that there were in the room five young men and one girl. The girl was Eileen, and three of the five young men held weapons. The weapons were the type that operated by induction. Near a wire, through which current was flowing, an electrical flow could also be induced in the little devices by pulling a trigger which merely made a connection between two plates. The induced current, thereupon, instantly discharged into whatever the instrument pointed at within 25 feet. The shock from one such weapon could jar a horse. And from three could kill a human being – and probably a Rull.

Deadly was the word. And so, reluctantly, he came further into the room. And then, at the command of a handsome young man with blond hair, pushed the door shut.

The blond man spoke again. 'I'm Dan,' he said. 'We've been checking into your background, Zeb. You're from one of the Sirius planet colonies?'

That was certainly the fact for the true Philip Zebner, and so there was no problem about admitting that.

'Zeb,' continued Dan, 'the destruction of that photographic plate ruined an $8,500,000 particle experiment. Eileen, after being sure it was you who destroyed it, decided she wasn't sure. So we want you to sign a confession.'

The realization had already come to the Rull that

these people also felt threatened by the destruction of the plate. And so, now again, that fateful act of his was once more feeding back trouble and confusion.

'Zeb,' continued the blond man, 'it'll take awhile before all this is settled. Meanwhile, if you leave the planet right away, we'll persuade Lowery to see that you get a degree. You can be safe in Sirius before there are any repercussions.

'I guess I have no choice,' agreed the Rull.

'Too bad in a way. I got kind of interested in you for our group when Eileen reported all that equipment you had in your closet. We can maybe use a guy with a bunch of destruct stuff, particularly now that we have all the connectors. Yeah,' he grinned, 'it won't work as it is. Where'd you take it? We looked, and it was gone.'

He could have blasted them all with his body energy. But there was a chance that one of them might have time to squeeze the transforming trigger.

The Rull said, 'Let's get the confession signed. That other stuff I hid when I discovered the connectors were missing. Forget about it!'

They were instantly accepting. And, after the new confession was signed, they trooped out in a friendly fashion. 'Goodbye, Zeb.' 'Have a good trip, Zeb!'

In a minute, he was alone. And beginning to feel better, himself. It was unfortunate that he couldn't remain to see what would happen when the two confessions were presented to the authorities. And unfortunate, in a way, that Lowery might lose his job. The man was a Rull asset, with his twisted method of teaching. Given the opportunity, and more time, he might successfully damage thousands more students of physics.

But the truth was, there were probably other Lowery types. And other communes getting passing grades for their members. This was the human race in daily life action.

The Zebner-Rull was back on the raft, as he had these thoughts. He was resigned now, to the human beings discovering that the raft was missing, but it no longer seemed like a menacing thing.

He had a prescient thought – that nobody on earth would guess that the mighty Rull enemy had come to their chief planet. Looked them over. And departed safely.

And that, in due course, the Rull would be back. In force.

# FOOTPRINT FARM

As THE car topped the hill, Peter Tasker felt the friendliness of the farm flowing up to meet him. He glanced at Evana in the seat beside him, hoping that she sensed it, also. He wanted to say eagerly, 'How does it look after two years?'

He didn't say it, of course. In the first place, the idea of a farm that reacted emotionally was a game that he played with himself. And in the second, Evana was sitting very straight, with her blue eyes fixed rigidly on the road ahead. Tasker turned to the back seat to see if nine-year-old Tiffy was looking. But she lay curled up, her face pressed against the cushion, apparently asleep. Tasker faced forward again. The judge had awarded Tiff to him for six months of each year, starting April 1. Today.

As they bowled along the fringe of the hill, the farm

spread below them, the footprint effect plainly visible. The 'sole,' a shallow, natural valley curved back to the green knoll of the 'arch,' on which stood the two-story farm house and its outbuildings. Beyond it, blurred now in the gathering twilight, was the rocky rim of the 'heel,' where the meteorite had fallen some four hundred years before, according to the testimony of experts he had sought out.

For the thousandth time, at least, Tasker visualized the fiery stone as it must have been on that far day, sweeping in low over the 'arch' and crashing into the resisting topsoil to form the heel of that giant footprint. There must have been echoing thunder in all the near valleys. Even a hundred miles away, the air had probably stirred and sighed and shivered as the vibrations of the impact recoiled in all directions simultaneously.

In his deposition for the court, Tasker had written:

'From my wife's accusations, we are expected to believe that, if Tiffy had continued to dig where those meteorite stones were found on our farm, she would eventually have run into something inimical. What form this – hostility – would take, she carefully refrains from mentioning, for, of course, it is nothing but a figment of her imagination. However, let us pursue her argument logically.'

At that point, supported by statements from scientists, he'd proved that no meteorite had ever contained bacteria, been radioactive, or chemically poisonous.

'Peter!' Evana's voice was sharp.

Tasker emerged from his reverie and realized she

144

had spoken more than once. He glanced at her quickly. Her color was high, and she was looking at him for the first time today.

'Peter, we've got to decide about me.'

Tasker shifted uneasily in his seat. He had gone to the city the day before, intending to try to persuade Evana to come with him and look after Tiffy during the six-month period. Before he could make the offer, she had said, 'Peter, I'll do anything if you let me come along.'

He'd started to say, 'But that's exactly –'

He stopped. There was a look in her face, a pale intensity of expression. Amazed, divining that she was offering a marriage relationship to her divorced husband, he stared at her. 'Anything?' he asked finally, wryly.

She nodded, but did not reply. Tasker shook his head wonderingly. 'My dear –' tenderly – 'you can come along without any special condition.'

'I'm offering one,' she had said then, stiffly, 'because I'm making one. Peter, I couldn't stand it if you let her dig.'

That chilled him. 'Evana,' he thought, 'it's only ground, it's only rock.' But he had known, even as the voiceless words repeated through his mind, that it would do no good to repeat them aloud. She had hated the farm from the beginning, a city-bred girl who would not, apparently could not, adjust.

As he guided the station wagon through the gate into the yard, he sighed and gave in. 'All right, you win. No digging.'

A minute later, he lifted the sleeping Tiffy out of the rear seat, and silently followed Evana towards the house.

To his surprise, the farm was content that night. 'Sleep!' it soothed him. And Tasker slept. When he wakened the next morning, he was astounded to see it was ten minutes after ten.

There was no sound from the other two bedrooms. 'City slickers!' Tasker murmured affectionately, as he dressed.

He spent the morning polishing small specimens of meteorite. By twelve o'clock his thoughts were elsewhere. Blonde Evana, slim and cheerful-looking in a bright blue gingham dress, looked around as he entered the kitchen. 'Tiffy's still asleep,' she said. 'I thought I'd let her get a good rest if she needed it.'

'Probably the change of air,' said Tasker.

Tasker spent the afternoon seeding the dry hilltop acreage. When he came in for dinner, Tiffy was just finishing her evening meal. It hadn't occurred to Tasker before that the girl might be fed separately. He wondered if Evana was trying to deny him his daughter's company.

Tiffy looked up and yawned. 'I don't know what's the matter, Daddy. I'm just so sleepy.'

Evana came in from the kitchen. 'She's going to bed right after dinner, aren't you dear?'

The explanations relaxed Tasker. The presence of these two warmed the room for him. 'That's what fresh air can do,' he said.

After Tiffy had been tucked away upstairs, Evana served dinner and said acidly, 'Don't keep repeating that fresh air gag. It makes you sound like a country hick.'

'Why not?' Tasker countered. 'That's what I am.'

'Don't be a fool.' She spoke curtly. She sounded as if it mattered to her.

The next day, also, Tiffy overslept. And the day after that. For the fourth morning, Tasker put an alarm clock in her room and stood by while it rang and rang. He shook her finally, gently at first, then more forcibly.

'Tiffy, wake up!'

She rolled loosely at his touch. He leaned closer, and called in her ear. She moved at that, and murmured: 'I'm so tired. Let me sleep.'

That made him choke up, and he had his first thought about taking her to a doctor.

Just before noon, he saw Tiffy out in the yard. She came, lackadaisically, to the workship in answer to his hail, a thin girl, tall for her age, her dark hair done up in bright pink ribbons.

She perked up a little as she gazed into the microscope at a piece of meteorite. 'Gee,' she said, 'it's all marked up.'

Her response revived Tasker's hope that he could interest her in his work. Five years before, he had been fired with an ambition to make a scientific study of what he still hoped would someday be recognized as the most unusual and interesting meteorite that had ever fallen on the planet. He explained, now, that the markings were the result of heat from friction, made centuries ago when the stone plunged from space. Tiffy nodded, gazed at several more specimens, and then turned away. 'I guess I've seen everything,' she said listlessly.

Tasker watched her go, uneasily.

A few minutes later, he glanced out of his workshop window and saw Tiffy taking a nap beside her dollhouse near the fence. Trembling, an unpleasant suspicion in his mind, Tasker went over to her.

'Tiffy!'

No answer.

Tenderly, he picked her up and carried her into the house. Evana held the door open for him, and he realized she must have watched the incident from the kitchen.

She led the way upstairs, swaying a little. After she had tucked Tiffy under the sheets, she turned abruptly on Tasker. 'This damned farm!' she said angrily.

His own suspicion was so all-enveloping now that Tasker felt sick. The bitter words came out before he could hold them back. 'Are you doping her?'

That stopped her fury as if he had struck her. The expression of pain that came into her face made her look like a hurt child. Suddenly, the sea blue of her eyes stirred and became discolored. She started to cry.

Tiffy slept on, her fingers balled into fists, her lank body loose under the quilt. Tasker gazed down at her, a lump in his throat, already convinced that his accusation was false.

'There's something wrong here,' he said huskily. 'It's foolish to believe it has anything to do with the meteorite. B-but I think we ought to take her to see Doctor Merrick – as soon as she wakes up.'

Tiffy danced into the doctor's private office, pirouetted past her father, and paused in front of the great oak desk. Her eyes shone brightly. She said in a shrill, cheerful voice:

'Doctor Merrick, I remember you.'

Doctor Merrick stood up. He was a well-dressed, alert man of forty, and his wide smile was friendly. 'Goodness,' he said, 'what a vivacious personality we have here.'

After his examination, he pulled the shining-eyed Tiffy in front of him and took her tightly closed hands in his with a quick, firm movement that startled Tasker because the girl resisted.

Resisted! Her body twisted ungracefully. Her face changed, grimaced, contorted, and her small teeth showed in an animallike snarl. Then, unable to free her hands from the doctor's tight grip, she dropped to her knees and bit savagely at his fingers.

In just moments, what had seemed a healthy child

had transformed into a thing that fought and mewled.

'Stop it!' said Tasker weakly.

He caught a glimpse of Evana's face, and the look on it made him half turn to prevent her from slipping off her chair in a faint. Before he could move to help her, Dr. Merrick's voice rose sternly above the bedlam.

'Hold the child!'

Tasker jumped forward. His hands, brutally strong with surprise, caught Tiffy by the shoulder and head. She writhed and jerked with astonishing strength, and her young face was twisted into an improbable mask of fury, but he held her.

Inexorably, the doctor forced open her hands. Tiffy screamed and then stood limp, her head drooping. All the resistance was gone from her. She looked suddenly like a very tired little girl.

'I thought so,' said Dr. Merrick. He gazed angrily at Tasker. 'What's the idea telling me she hasn't been doing any digging?'

'But she hasn't.' Tasker spoke automatically. 'We've kept her under constant –'

He stopped, choking a little. Tears of pity welled up in his eyes. 'Tiffy, darling,' he said, 'your hands.'

How she had kept them hidden from Evana and himself, Tasker could not even guess. They were raw, and bleeding slightly. There were blisters on both palms that would have made a grown man cringe in agony. As he bandaged those poor, torn hands, the doctor spoke quietly.

'Her reflexes were too slow ... Outwardly, so bright and peppy, but her nerves and muscles reacted as if she were on the point of exhaustion. And then, fortunately, I caught a glimpse of her right palm ... I'd like your wife to take her into the anteroom while you and I have a talk, Mr. Tasker.'

After the door had closed behind mother and daughter, Tasker said, 'I don't understand it. She was under constant observation.'

'At night, too?'

'But that's impossible,' Tasker said sharply. 'You can't believe that she would sneak out in the dark and –'

He stopped in a wondering belief. 'But, of course, that's why she slept so late.'

He stood up, trembling. Before he could speak, Doctor Merrick said something about taking Tiffy to see a psychiatrist. Other phrases came through. 'Traumatic experience.' 'Compulsion neurosis.'

Tasker's mind brushed the words aside. To him, the advice was meaningless. He felt himself on the edge of an abyss, but he had no desire to resist the thoughts that came. Evana had been right. How she had guessed the truth was a matter too intricate to be thought about now. Her fears of the meteorite, seen in this new light, showed sensitivity of the first order and more than human awareness of something that was not human. And he had believed he was the logical one.

He said aloud, 'We'll do that, Doctor. I'll drive Evana and Tiffy to the city today, and then –'

He stopped. He had a feeling that if he didn't watch out he'd babble to the physician that he was returning to the farm alone that night – for what? He wasn't sure. What was it that was buried under the 'heel' of Footprint Farm? Whatever it was, it was up to him, alone, to find it. No time, now, to start persuading other people. It had taken him nearly five years to realize a truth that Evana had sensed in her first weeks at the farm. He felt unutterably humble before that simple fact.

It was after midnight when, having taken Evana

and Tiffy home, he drove back into the farmyard. He went upstairs, and as he crept wearily into bed he was thinking *Tomorrow – I'll go out there and dig – tomorrow –*

He woke blurrily to the sound of the phone ringing, and the thought *The farm doesn't want me to answer that*. He was slipping off into slumber again when it struck him how fantastic that was.

'Of course I'll answer,' he told himself with a yawn. 'No!'

He yielded, impressed by the tremendousness of his fatigue. But just as he started to sleep, the phone, which had been briefly silent, began to ring again. That woke him. He sat up, blinking, utterly appalled. Full-grown, the truth burst upon him. *Something out there is trying to make me sleep. The notion I've had all these years of a personified farm wasn't a game I was playing. It was a game that was being played on me.*

The cunning of it was simple enough, but it implied an unhuman danger. Yet, swiftly, he realized that the new development had favorable aspects. The hands of his watch pointed at five minutes after three, and so not too much time had gone by.

Downstairs, the phone was ringing again. Moments later, after a mad dash, Tasker picked up the receiver with trembling fingers, and gasped hello. And heard Evana's voice at the other end.

'What's the matter with you?' She sobbed and talked at the same time. 'I've been calling you for hours. Peter, she's gone. Tiffy, I mean. She must have gone back to the farm with you. She must have hidden herself in all that stuff you have in the back of your station wagon. Is she there? Did you find her? Peter, stop her! Stop her from digging!'

Her incoherent words, when he finally understood

151

them, made him tensely calm.

'Evana, I'll go out there. I'll call you back.'

'No, wait, wait! I am not at home. I'm on the road. I'll be there in three hours.'

He ran out the door and across his porch, and then hesitated because he couldn't recall if he had hung up the receiver. He actually had to fight that orderliness in him that made him want to go back to make sure. Across the yard he raced, and across the pasture toward the 'heel.' Cautiously, he approached the edge of the steep incline, and then he was gazing over the rim. As he saw the vague movement in the darkness below. He stopped.

She was digging in the night, under a moon that was like an inverted saucer hanging low in the western sky. Digging quietly and steadily, with a spade in a hole that, even in the shadows of that indentation, seemed large and deep.

Kneeling there, Tasker pitied Tiffy, whose mind and body had been taken over by an alien spirit that frantically overstrained her muscles and strength in order to achieve its own purpose.

Tasker started down the hill. Without hesitation, he jumped into the hole beside Tiffy and tenderly took the small spade from her fingers. She offered no resistance. He felt her shiver as he picked her up and carried her back up the hill and towards the house.

Upstairs in the bathroom, he removed the tattered, dirty bandages that Doctor Merrick had put on her hands the previous afternoon. Gently, he washed those tortured hands and gently bound them again. And then he carried her down the stairs and out to the garage and put her into the front seat of the station wagon. He selected a sledge hammer, a pick, and a shovel. A minute later, the headlights were glaring a pathway back to the 'heel.' Tasker was trying to imagine what the thing would be like, and what he would have to do to destroy it, when the little girl said softly,

'What are you intending to do?'

He glanced at her with wide, startled eyes. 'My God,' he thought, 'it's talking to me through her.'

He stopped the car. Before he could speak, Tiffy said:

'All these years I've wanted only freedom. I tried to persuade every person that came this way to dig me up, but it was too hard to control the bigger ones. So with you, I tried the method of making you want to remain here –'

'While you,' said Tasker, 'took over the body of a helpless child, and overstrained every muscle in her body. No matter what happens now, she has been permanently damaged.'

'I'm sure you're wrong. But I tried to be careful. I had her sleep long hours, but I admit I knew nothing about blisters.'

That penetrated. It seemed true. How could so utterly different a being know about human limitations?

'Why didn't you try to talk to us through her sooner?'

Her secrecy he could understand. Tiffy would not know that she was possessed. She would only be aware that she was doing wrong in going out at night to dig, and so in the secretive way of children, she would keep her own counsel.

'Before she went away, I could only control her in the simplest physical way. She seems to have changed.'

Tasker was trying to think of how to explain about human beings growing older when Tiffy said, 'What are you afraid of?'

Her eyes gazed back at him steadily, and in the light from the dashboard they were serene blue in color, calm and with depths unfathomable. And he knew that it did not merely mean afraid, now. The question struck to the roots of his being. It was as if a stone had been dropped into the well of time inside him and the echo had come from a million years, an ancestral sound of many vibrations.

He had a vision of himself as the descendant of a continuous line of ten-thousand parents, from the day that man had climbed to his feet and looked up at the stars and reached for the near sky. With such a background, what was he afraid of?

Why, of the night, and of the unknown! Of darkness and the river, of thunder and lightning, and of the strange gleams of purpose in the eyes of other men. He was afraid of nameless things, and – shameful – afraid of himself.

It did not occur to him to speak again. He slipped the machine into low gear and guided the truck down the steep road he had once used for carting rocks. Twisting down, and then a quick, sharp turn and the emergency brake did the rest. The headlights poured their brightness into the four-foot hole that Tiffy had dug in the hard, rocky earth.

It was an hour later, when the eastern sky was already thick with light, that he struck a piece of rock that clanged almost like metal. He spaded the soil away from its gleaming sides, and was energetically marking off its limits, when his shovel abruptly went through into a deeper hole. As he jerked it back, startled, he knocked loose more of the dirt, making a cavity several inches in diameter.

He was still off-balance, then, as he saw the movement at the bottom of the hole. A shadowy object wiggled up toward the dawn light. Twice it tried to lift itself up, but it was too large for the opening.

'Wait!' said Tasker shakily. 'Get back!'

The uneasy thrill of the first seeing of the thing was fading. The dawn was brighter. The ground felt firm and hard, and gave him a sense of normalcy. He looked down into the darkness of the hole and the unexpectedly small size of the thing that was there made him feel better about his decision to release it.

'Get out of the way!' he said. 'I'll enlarge the opening.'

'Quick!' said Tiffy from just behind him. 'She's coming.'

'She?' Tasker echoed, uncomprehendingly.

There was the sound of a car motor from beyond the hill. The sound ceased. A door slammed. A scrambling sound. And then Evana appeared on the rim, silhouetted against the bright sky.

Tasker's voice rose on the clear air, 'Evana, come down here and get Tiffy. I'm about to let the thing go.'

The woman let out an inarticulate cry and came running, stumbling, down the slope. Twice, she fell. But each time she made it back to her feet almost at once. And then she was down in the excavation, and had snatched Tiffy in her arms.

'Sweetheart, are you all right?'

'Evana,' said Tasker in a strained voice, 'please hurry! Go back to the house! I'm sure you don't want to be around when it comes out.'

Evana released Tiffy slightly. Relaxed her tight grip, was more the way it was. She stared at Tasker and her voice had a puzzled note in it as she said, 'You mean, you've actually got something down there.'

At that point, his words must finally have penetrated. Her face drained of color. 'Before – it – comes – out,' she echoed. 'Why, you madman, you've got to kill it.'

Before he could realize her intent, she lunged at him, her teeth showing and hit him with the full weight of her body. It was so unexpected, it threw him off-balance. And so, as she grabbed the spade, he let go of it.

She couldn't have had any plan, for her first thrust with the shovel widened the hole to more than a foot. Bare moments after that, Tasker had recovered. And now he did the lunging. She was five feet six, probably a hundred and twenty pounds, and every ounce of that weight seemed to have muscles that squirmed and fought. It was a battle from the instant he grabbed her, and every inch of the way he carried her. But he was strong from years of physical labor. And so, after a minute, he had her out of the pit.

As he literally dumped her to the ground, he said, harshly, 'Take Tiffy to the house! There's nothing here for you, in your state of mind. This is contact with an alien intelligence; something fantastic and wonderful that lives on meteorites, or in them. Don't you see?'

He saw that she didn't. But she did look blank and continued to lie on the ground. Hastily, he turned back to get Tiffy.

She was down in the pit, pulling the shovel out of the hole. She stepped back.

The thing that floated up out of the shadows seemed to be made of dark, opaque glass. Like the eyes of a fly, it presented thousands of surfaces to the light. Its beauty was the beauty of an enormous cut emerald, for as it emerged into the open, it turned green. It shimmered, seemed to hesitate, then floated higher. As it drew near Tiffy, it swerved and momentarily caressed her cheek. She laughed the laughter of a delighted child, and touched the green surface with her bandaged hands.

In the east the sun, though still below the horizon, cast up a pall of red light that lit up the whole sky.

Like a thistledown now, the thing mounted upwards. A hundred feet up, it floated into the rays of the rising sun. It jumped as if it had been struck. Like a shooting star, it darted into the sky. Faster it moved. Brighter it gleamed. It became a tiny, shining thing at the remote edge of vision. It twinkled. And was gone.

Tasker was aware of Evana sobbing softly. 'Oh, Task,' she said, unconsciously using her old nickname of endearment for him, 'it was so beautiful.'

Tiffy, he saw then, had an intent look on her small, up-turned face. 'Daddy – Mum – when it touched me, it said it will ... come ... back as soon as – I don't quite understand – something about the discovery of live things like us on a planet would be a complete surprise to – to –' She fumbled verbally. 'I don't quite get it.'

Tasker took three firm steps over to Evana and placed his arm around her unresisting shoulder. He guided her over to Tiffy, and drew her, also unresisting, into the embrace of his left arm.

'Let's go,' he said, '... home.'

# THE NON-ARISTOTELIAN
# DETECTIVE

Detective, using non-Aristotelian methods, will take interesting cases. Particularly want unsolved murders and other major crimes which have baffled police. No charge, fee, or expense of any description, but client must be in position to give me entry into the situation. Find address through telephone number.

DETECTIVE LIEUTENANT Myron Morrison read the advertisement with a choleric amusement. There was a self-confidence about the wording that irritated him. He looked up, finally, at Inspector Codreau, who had brought the want ad column in to show to him.

'What in blazes,' he demanded, 'is a non-Arist –' He stumbled – 'Non-Aristlelian detective?'

Codreau's broad face creased into a grin. 'I'm like you,' he said, 'I can't even pronounce it.' He sighed, and shook his head. 'I guess we're just a couple of out-of-date dicks.'

Morrison was studying the advertisement again. 'So he'll take cases that have baffled the police, will he?' He was more annoyed than he cared to admit.

'The word's not in Webster's,' said the inspector. 'I looked it up.'

'What do you want me to do? Check on him?'

'Hmmm. Hadn't really thought about it. I just saw it in the paper and I thought you'd be interested.' He broke off. 'Anything else about the ad strike you?'

Morrison read it through slowly. He was about to shake his head, puzzled, when he got it. 'Well,' he said, 'no phone number.' He grew thoughtful. He leaned back and scratched his head, a big man in a gray suit. He said, 'Say-y-y, to get in touch with him you've got to figure out how you'd locate his phone number and address when he doesn't give either.'

'The newspaper would give us the information.'

Morrison agreed that undoubtedly it could be as simple as that. Frowning, he studied the advertisement again and then reached for the phone. 'You don't mind,' he said to Codreau.

Morrison dialed Information, hesitated, then asked, 'Have you a listing under Non-Aristot-tatelian detective?'

Moments later, he had the phone number and was dialing again. This time it was an answering service. He repeated his question, picked up a pencil, grinned at Codreau, and said, 'I want his name and address.'

He hung up moments later, said, 'There we are. Philip Nicer, 721 Glen Oak Crescent. That's one of those lost streets in the hills, I think.'

'Anyway,' said the inspector, 'He's within our jurisdiction.'

'Yes,' said Morrison grimly, 'and I know just the case I'll take along with me. Remember that Mrs. Nina Colton murder five years ago?'

'Vaguely.' Codreau looked blank, then, 'Good lord, man, you're not going to –'

'If he can solve cases that have baffled the police,' Morrison said placidly, 'we might as well get the benefit of his non-Aristot –' he gave it up, snarled, 'At least, I'll learn how to pronounce it and maybe even find out what it means.'

The inspector's brown eyes were serious. 'Before you let outraged pride carry you off the deep end, why don't you look over the file record of the Colton case again and then decide if you really want to do this?'

It was an obviously good idea, and Morrison went off. When he came back half an hour later, he said, 'It's just as I remember it. I'd like your opinion. Do you have time?'

The body of Mrs. Colton had been found in her bedroom, completely nude, a bullet in her heart. Her husband, a real-estate salesman, had been out on a business call and had spent the evening with a couple previously unknown to him, who had vouched for his being with them from about nine o'clock until shortly after eleven.

A scream and the sound of a shot had brought neighbors into the Colton house a few minutes after ten, and there they found Mrs. Colton breathing her last. She died without regaining consciousness as the police were arriving.

After a neighbor of the Coltons reported having once seen him and Mrs. Colton in a significant act – kissing – Ivan Tristrov, the dead woman's husband's real-estate associate had confessed having been her lover for about a year. However, he swore that Mrs. Colton had ended the relationship on the grounds that it was her husband she really loved.

Tristrov had spent the entire evening and night of the murder with his wife and another couple. His wife had subsequently divorced him, because of his confessed infidelity. Tristrov took the divorce badly.

Although the gun that had killed Mrs. Colton was her husband's, and was found lying beside the body, the police were convinced that she had not committed suicide. There were no powder marks on her skin, which indicated that the bullet had been fired from a distance greater than any one person could have managed.

A check back on the couple who had been entertained by the Tristrovs the night of the murder had established the man as being a close friend. In fact, Tristrov had cosigned a note for him a few weeks earlier for a large sum. The woman and Mrs. Tristrov were chums. While the two women prepared sandwiches, the men went out for a short walk, but were not gone more than ten minutes, everybody had sworn.

Friends and neighbors testified to Mr. Colton's good character. He was not a man who chased women, and seemed to have been unaware of his wife's affair with his partner.

After Morrison had concluded his summary of the five-year-old murder, Inspector Codreau nodded. 'I remember I always felt Colton was not as unaware of his wife's infidelity as was made out. And so, in spite of his apparent airtight alibi, I really figured he did it.'

Morrison said, 'At the time, I believed it was Mrs. Tristrov. After all, her only alibi for what she was doing when the two men went out for a walk was her best friend. And everybody knows that a woman will lie into your face without blinking an eye if she thinks it's a good cause. And what better cause could this friend have than to help another woman against an unfaithful husband's mistress?'

He continued, 'Besides, there's the fact that Mrs. Tristrov was so bitter afterwards, and persisted in divorcing her husband in spite of his pleading. Any woman with that much hatred –' He stopped. 'Well, that's my view.'

The inspector had relaxed and his eyes were suddenly twinkling. 'Are you in a position to give Mr. Nicer entry into the situation, as required by the ad?'

The big man frowned. 'Since, naturally, I'll handle this on my own time, I guess if I tell who the people are, and other details, that'll be giving him a pretty good in.'

Later that day, as he was finally on his way out of the building, Detective Lieutenant Morrison noticed that two reporters were drooping over a table in the press room. He went in.

'Say,' he said, 'is either of you a college man? I ought to know better than to ask a question like that, but I'm a credulous fellow when it comes to reporters. I just have a feeling sometimes that they know everything.'

'What do you want to know?' That was Carler, a creature of the Lawton Press, sleek, weary-looking, pallid-complexioned.

'Go on!' scoffed Morrison. 'Not you. You can't even spell.'

'So help me,' said Carler, 'I was in for four years. And just because I misspelled your name once –'

'Okay, okay. What does non-Aristotelian mean? Say –,' Wonderingly –, 'it sounded right that time.'

'It's got something to do with semantics,' said Carler.

'With what?' Morrison was outraged by the introduction of another word that he didn't know.

Carler spelled it for him. 'Has to do with the

meaning of meaning,' he said. 'I remember they were going to introduce it into the English and Psychology classes the year after I left college.'

'You mean there's actually something in this business?' Morrison was disturbed.

Carler said, 'Lots of colleges teach it now. What's the gag?'

Morrison considered it inadvisable to tell the truth so he said, 'Remember that Colton woman murder, five years ago. You were on it.'

'Yes. I always figured Tristrov did it. We hear about these hot-blooded Latins, but what about the hot-headed Slavs. I think he killed her for throwing him over.'

The second reporter, Tom James, piped up. 'My own feeling was that the police should have accepted the suicide theory. The way Tristrov described it, that woman was ridden by guilt, remorse, and shame. Don't underestimate true feelings like that.'

Morrison groaned, 'Everybody understands human behavior on the basis of some personal philosophy. No wonder crime goes merrily along. Goodbye.'

Twenty minutes later, as he climbed towards Glen Oak Crescent, Morrison felt his car presently shift into low gear. The street wound steeply upward, finally, grudgingly leveled off. But before he reached the top, a sadness came over Morrison. He recognized the district. It had been built up about twelve years before. It had been an expensive, exclusive development then, and prices had been going up ever since.

Boy, oh, boy, had he ever let himself into the pit. Well, he'd just have to act casual.

The house he wanted was a long-fronted, two-story structure on a deep lot. A young man was backing a brown Cadillac out of an archway at one end of the house. As Morrison parked his own car and climbed out, the big machine came bowling along backward. It turned onto the street, and wheeled toward where the detective lieutenant was standing.

Morrison had a sudden idea that this was his man, and the possibility that he might miss making contact galvanized him. He waved, the driver saw him, drew up at the curb opposite, leaned over, peered through the turned-down window, and said, 'Why, hello, Lieutenant Morrison. My name is Nicer. Do you want to see me?'

Morrison was caught off guard. 'How in blazes do you –?' he began. He stopped, startled. He had been about to ask the how-do-you-know-who-I-am question. He clamped his teeth together. Sherlock Holmes stuff, eh? And he in the role of the mystified, admiring, dumb cop.

He stood, inwardly smoldering at the narrowness of his escape. But after a moment he shrugged. The truth was, he had nothing to lose and he was curious.

'All right, how do you know my name?'

A pair of sardonic gray eyes and a middle-thirties face grinned at him. 'I'll tell you after I've solved your case. I can tell you the cards were heavily stacked in my favor.'

He opened the door of the car. 'I'm on my way down to the boulevard for a minute. Would you care to come along? We can talk en route.'

– An engaging guy, perhaps a little over-confident. But there was a stern look around his eyes. No kid, this.

Morrison climbed in. Then, when they were moving, 'Look, Mr. Nicer, what's all this non-Aristota –?' He stopped, defeated.

Nicer grinned at him. 'That damned word,' he said, 'is pronounced NON-arIStoTELian. It derives from Aristotle, the famous Greek philosopher of long ago.

It means not like Aristotle.'

Morrison couldn't remember what Aristotle was famous for, and so naturally had no idea what non-Aristotle would be. And, particularly, he wanted to know what would a non-Aristotle-type detective do that was different.

Nicer explained that there were many non-Aristotelian systems, but a non-Aristotelian detective would be one who used the seven levels of logic as defined by *General Semantics*, adhering strictly to a line of reasoning that derived from Korzybski's Ladder of Abstraction.

'For example,' said Nicer, 'a criminal is a person who would have a poor method of making the referent fit the territory.'

Morrison considered that unhappily. He was an old-style detective with a high school education and a number of special courses. He was perfectly aware that in today's big city police departments, someone like him coming in new would get nowhere. He was not outdated. With his formidable experience, that was not a factor. But along with Codreau, and other aging experts, his type would eventually be retired out of existence.

– What in ... was a referent, anyway? Reluctantly, he asked the question.

'It's a map,' said Nicer, 'But in the GS – general semantic – meaning, it's in the person's mind. A map, as you know, is an abstraction, a sketch, a summary, a synopsis of a real geographical area, a real object, a creature, or a genuine process in Nature. It is never the area, object, creature, or process. A photograph of a man, however good a likeness, gives only a partial picture of the reality.'

Morrison was minded to say, 'So what? I've known that all my life.' But he didn't say it. If a hundred or more universities were teaching stuff like that now, the unfavorable reaction of Detective Lieutenant Myron Morrison was unimportant. He shifted in the seat, saw that they were on the main boulevard, hesitated, and then asked the vital question, 'What has that got to do with finding a murderer?'

Nicer said, 'Viewed semantically, every situation is different. So tell me the exact case that you have in mind –'

Since he had taken the trouble to come, Morrison gave the details of the Colton murder correctly.

By the time the account was finished, Nicer was pulling into a parking lot behind a drug store. He got out. 'Be right back,' he said.

During the eight minutes that he had to wait, Morrison thought *I suppose I could say that this is what a professional gets when he comes to an amateur.* But truth was, he was interested. He thought *There's no way out for Nicer.*

Incredibly, the younger man had talked himself into the pit ... *He's got to come through.*

Nicer emerged from the store with a package, climbed into the car, started it, and drove back the way he had come. At this point, he asked one question about the Colton case: 'Did any of the principals in this matter ever, that you know of, physically assault either a man or a woman for any reason?'

Morrison told him yes, told him who.

When he had the answer, Nicer was silent. The car wound up the steep hill. Abruptly, he apologized and explained, 'I was just going over the facts again as you gave them to me, and there's no question; the-map-is-not-the-territory aspect of non-Aristotelian logic fits this particular murder.'

He finished, 'No question, there's your murderer.'

Morrison hadn't vaguely expected a solution on the

basis of reasoning alone. He had taken it for granted they would revisit the five-year-old scenes, see again Colton, Tristrov and wife as they now were, and the other people. The surprise was so complete that his mind seemed to career. 'Huh!' he said, 'you're kidding.'

He remembered the facile analyses of the two reporters, of Codreau, and of, frankly, himself. He thought gloomily *Everybody's an armchair detective these days*.

Before he could speak, the handsome young man said, with a faint, sympathetic smile, 'What you're listening to is non-Aristotelian reasoning.'

He thereupon enlarged upon his previously stated concept, to the effect that human beings operated on mental maps based on a preconceived emotional rigidity. People became disturbed when the life situation did not fit their mental map. Hence, in a murder, a non-Aristotelian detective must decide which element, or combination of elements, of general semantic logic applied – in this instance, the map-territory concept – and then discover whose mental map was sufficiently at variance with reality to cause him to react with the infinite violent intent of a person who was then capable of snuffing out the life of another living person.

'Yes,' groped Morrison, 'but Tristrov hit his wife because she left him. He went to her sister's, where she was staying, and beat her up, but good. When we picked him up, he was crying like a baby. He said he'd promised her he'd never misbehave again. But when she wouldn't listen, he just lost control of himself and started to hit her because she had made him feel so bad. I kind've felt sorry for him, because you know the world isn't like women think –'

He stopped. 'Hey,' he said slowly, 'you mean his

map was that she ought to forgive him, and when her response didn't fit his map, he –'

'Exactly,' said Philip Nicer. 'He went berserk and tried to beat her brains out. Please understand me, not all men who hit women reach the point of murder, but since a murder occurred in that frame –' He broke off, 'Well, here we are back at your car.'

He drew up behind Morrison's Chevy. Morrison climbed heavily out of the Cadillac and stood towering beside it. He was thinking hard; it was the most convincing analysis to date. He said, 'All right, let's say Tristrov did it. But how can we pin it on him? He'd laugh at us if we pulled him in.'

The man in the car smiled grimly. 'Once you have your teeth into a case, I've always found that you can reason backwards by ordinary logic. Now, think. The alibi situation in that murder is so great it can't just have happened. Tristrov had to make preparations. So I'll simply point out that when Tristrov cosigned his friend's note, that was the key act. I'll wager he expected that the man would be satisfied with the cosigning. But put yourself in that man's place; suddenly you realize that you have been cunningly made an accessory to a murder. End of friendship, right? And so –'

'Tristrov had to pay off the note!' Morrison said explosively. 'If that checks out, Mister, then –' he finished plaintively, 'but why did he kill Mrs. Colton?'

'You'll have to ask him that when you question him,' said Nicer. 'I think he'll confess because, remember, when he was confronted with having been seen kissing Mrs. Colton, he admitted having been her lover, which he needn't have done. So he can lose his head ... My own belief would be that Mrs. Colton intended to tell her husband about the affair and ask his forgiveness which, of course, would ruin Tristrov across the board. That happened anyway, but the resultant confusion saved him until now. That's it, Lieutenant. The credit, if any, is all yours. Call me any time during the next month. I'm on leave from the European branch of Military Intelligence, and I'd like to see what other aspects of non-Aristotelian logic show up in major crimes – like to see it in a practice environment where, hopefully, I don't get killed if I'm wrong.'

'What about – your knowing my name?'

Nicer grinned. 'Military Intelligence has a picture gallery of all sergeant-up police officers in the metropolitan area. I looked over the photos of the men in this district. Told you it was stacked.'

It was next day. Inspector Codreau was waiting for Morrison when he came in. 'That bank phoned while you were out,' he said. 'Tristrov paid off that note. I'm having him brought in for questioning ...'

# THE HUMAN OPERATORS

Written in collaboration with
**HARLAN ELLISON**

SHIP: THE only place.

Ship says I'm to get wracked today at noon. And so I'm in grief already.

It seems unfair to have to get wracked three whole days ahead of the usual once-a-month. But I learned long ago not to ask Ship to explain anything personal.

I sense today is different; some things are happening. Early, I put on the spacesuit and go outside – which is not common. But a screen got badly scored by meteor dust; and I'm here, now, replacing it. Ship would say I'm being bad because, as I do my job, I sneak quick looks around me. I wouldn't dare do it in the forbidden places inside. I noticed when I was still a kid that Ship doesn't seem to be so much aware of what I do when I'm outside.

And so I carefully sneak a few looks at the deep

black space. And at the stars.

I once asked Ship why we never go toward those points of brilliance, those stars, as Ship calls them. For that question, I got a whole extra wracking, and a long, ranting lecture about how all those stars have humans living on their planets, and of how vicious humans are. Ship really blasted me that time, saying things I'd never heard before, like how Ship had gotten away from the vicious humans during the big war with the Kyben. And how, every once in a long while, Ship has a 'run-in' with the vicious humans but the defractor perimeter saves us. I don't know what Ship means by all that; I don't even know what a 'run-in' is, exactly.

The last 'run-in' must have been before I was big enough to remember. Or, at least, before Ship killed my father when I was fourteen. Several times, when he was still alive, I slept all day for no reason that I can think of. But since I've been doing all the maintenance work – since age fourteen – I sleep only my regular six-hour night. Ship tells me night and Ship tells me day, too.

I kneel here in my spacesuit, feeling tiny on this gray and curving metal place in the dark. Ship is big. Over five hundred feet long, and about a hundred and fifty feet thick at the widest back there. Again, I have that special out-here thought: suppose I just give myself a shove, and float right off toward one of those bright spots of light? Would I be able to get away? I think I would like that; there has to be someplace else than Ship.

As in the past, I slowly and sadly let go of the idea. Because if I try, and Ship catches me, I'll *really* get wracked.

The repair job is finally done. I clomp back to the airlock, and use the spider to dilate it, and let myself be sucked back into what is, after all – I've got to admit it – a pretty secure place. All the gleaming corridors, the huge storerooms with their equipment and spare parts, and the freezer rooms with their stacks of food (enough, says Ship, to last one person for centuries), and the deck after deck of machinery that it's my job to keep in repair. I can take pride in that. *'Hurry! It is six minutes to noon!'* Ship announces. I'm hurrying now.

I strip off my spacesuit and stick it to the decontamination board and head for the wracking room. At least, that's what *I* call it. I suppose it's really part of the engine room on Underdeck Ten, a special chamber fitted with electrical connections, most of which are testing instruments. I use them pretty regularly in my work. My father's father's father installed them for Ship, I think I recall.

There's a big table, and I climb on top of it and lie down. The table is cold against the skin of my back and butt and thighs, but it warms me up as I lie here. It's now one minute to noon. As I wait, shuddering with expectation, the ceiling lowers toward me. Part of what comes down fits over my head, and I feel the two hard knobs pressing into the temples of my skull. And cold; I feel the clamps coming down over my middle, my wrists, my ankles. A strap with metal in it tightens flexibly but firmly across my chest.

*'Ready!'* Ship commands.

It always seems bitterly unfair. How can I ever be ready to be wracked? I hate it! Ship counts: *'Ten ... nine ... eight ... one!'*

The first jolt of electricity hits and everything tries to go in different directions; it feels like someone is tearing something soft inside me – that's the way it feels.

Blackness swirls into my head and I forget

177

everything. I am unconscious for a while. Just before I regain myself, before I am finished and Ship will permit me to go about my duties, I remember a thing I have remembered many times. This isn't the first time for this memory. It is of my father and a thing he said once, not long before he was killed. 'When Ship says vicious, Ship means smarter. There are ninety-eight other chances.'

He said those words very quickly. I think he knew he was going to get killed soon. Oh, of course, he *must* have known, my father must, because I was nearly fourteen then, and when *he* had become fourteen, Ship had killed *his* father, so he must have known.

And so the words are important. I know that; they are important; but I don't know what they mean, not completely.

*'You are finished!'* Ship says.

I get off the table. The pain still hangs inside my head and I ask Ship, 'Why am I wracked three days earlier than usual?'

Ship sounds angry. *'I can wrack you again!'*

But I know Ship won't. Something new is going to happen and Ship wants me whole and alert for it. Once, when I asked Ship something personal, right after I was wracked, Ship did it again, and when I woke up Ship was worrying over me with the machines. Ship seemed concerned I might be damaged. Ever after that, Ship has not wracked me twice close together. So I ask, not really thinking I'll get an answer, but I ask just the same.

*'There is a repairing I want you to do!'*

Where, I ask. *'In the forbidden part below!'*

I try not to smile. I knew there was a new thing going to happen and this is it. My father's words come back again. *Ninety-eight other chances.*

Is this one of them?

I descend in the dark. There is no light in the dropshaft, Ship says I need no light. But I know the truth. Ship does not want me to be able to find my way back here again. This is the lowest I've ever been in Ship.

So I drop steadily, smoothly, swiftly. Now I come to a slowing place and slower and slower, and finally my feet touch the solid deck and I am here.

Light comes on. Very dimly, I move in the direction of the glow, and Ship is with me, all around me, of course. Ship is always with me, even when I sleep. Especially when I sleep.

The glow gets brighter as I round a curve in the corridor, and I see it is caused by a round panel that blocks the passage, touching the bulkheads on all sides, flattened at the bottom to fit the deckplates. It looks like glass, that glowing panel. I walk up to it and stop. There is no place else to go.

*'Step through the screen!'* Ship says.

I take a step toward the glowing panel but it doesn't slide away into the bulkhead as so many other panels that *don't* glow slide. I stop.

*'Step through!'* Ship tells me again.

I put my hands out in front of me, palms forward, because I am afraid if I keep walking I will bang my nose against the glowing panel. But as my fingers touch the panel they seem to get soft, and I can see a light yellow glow through them, as if they are transparent. And my hands go *through* the panel and I can see them faintly, glowing yellow, on the other side. Then my naked forearms, then I'm right up against the panel, and my face goes through and everything is much lighter, more yellow, and I step onto the other side, in a forbidden place Ship has never allowed me to see.

I hear voices. They are all the same voice, but they

are talking to one another in a soft, running-together way, the way I sound when I am just talking to myself sometimes in my cubicle with my cot in it.

I decide to listen to what the voices are saying, but not to ask Ship about them, because I think it *is* Ship talking to itself, down here in this lonely place. I will think about what Ship is saying later, when I don't have to make repairs and act the way Ship wants me to act. What Ship is saying to itself is interesting.

This place does not look like other repair places I know in Ship. It is filled with so many great round glass balls on pedestals, each giving off its yellow light in pulses, that I cannot count them. There are rows and rows of clear glass balls, and inside them I see metal ... and other things, soft things all together. And the wires spark gently, and the soft things move, and the yellow light pulses. I think these glass balls are what are talking. But I don't if that's so. I only *think* it is.

Two of the glass balls are dark. Their pedestals look chalky, not shining white like all the others. Inside the two dark balls, there are black things like burned-out wires. The soft things don't move.

'*Replace the overloaded modules!*' Ship says.

I know Ship means the dark globes. So I go over to them and I look at them and after a while I say, yes, I can repair these, and Ship says it knows I can, and to get to it quickly. Ship is hurrying me; something is going to happen. I wonder what it will be?

I find replacement globes in a dilation chamber, and I take the sacs off them and do what has to be done to make the soft things move and the wires spark, and I listen very carefully to the voices whispering and warming each other with words as Ship talks to itself, and I hear a great many things that don't mean anything to me because they are speaking about things that happened before I was born, and about parts of Ship I've never seen. But I hear a great many things that I *do* understand, and I know Ship would never let me hear these things if it wasn't absolutely necessary for me to be here repairing the globes. I remember all these things.

Particularly the part where Ship is crying.

When I have the globes repaired and now all of them are sparking and pulsing and moving, Ship asks me, '*Is the intermind total again!*'

So I say yes it is, and Ship says get upshaft, and I go soft through that glowing panel and I'm back in the passage. I go back to the dropshaft and go up, and Ship tells me, '*Go to your cubicle and make yourself clean!*'

I do it, and decide to wear a clothes, but Ship says be naked, and then says, '*You are going to meet a female!*' Ship has never said that before. I have never seen a female.


It is because of the female that Ship sent me down to the forbidden place with the glowing yellow globes, the place where the intermind lives. And it is because of the female that I am waiting in the dome chamber linked to the airlock. I am waiting for the female to come across from – I will have to understand this – *another* ship. Not *Ship*, the Ship I know, but some *other* ship with which Ship has been in communication. I did not know there were other ships.

I had to go down to the place of the intermind, to repair it, so Ship could let this other ship get close without being destroyed by the defractor perimeter. Ship has not told me this; I overheard it in the intermind place, the voices talking to one another. The voices said, '*His father was vicious!*'

I know what that means. My father told me when

Ship says vicious, Ship means smarter. Are there ninety-eight other ships? Are those the ninety-eight other chances? I hope that's the answer, because many things are happening all at once, and my time may be near at hand. My father did it, broke the globe mechanism that allowed Ship to turn off the defractor perimeter, so other ships could get close. He did it many years ago, and Ship did without it for all those years rather than trust me to go to the intermind, to overhear all that I've heard. But now Ship needs to turn off the perimeter so the other ship can send the female across. Ship and the other ship have been in communication. The human operator on the other ship is a female, my age. She is going to be put aboard Ship and we are to produce one and, maybe later on, another human child. I know what that means. When the child reaches fourteen, I will be killed.

The intermind said while she's 'carrying' a human child, the female does not get wracked by her ship. If things do not come my way, perhaps I will ask Ship if *I* can 'carry' the human child; then I won't be wracked at all. And I have found out why I was wracked three days ahead of time. The female's period – whatever that is; I don't think I have one of those – ended last night. Ship has talked to the other ship and the thing they don't seem to know is what the 'fertile time' is. I don't know, either, otherwise I would try and use that information. But all it seems to mean is that the female will be put aboard Ship every day till she gets another 'period.'

It will be nice to talk to someone besides Ship.

I hear the high sound of something screaming for a long drawn-out time and I ask Ship what it is. Ship tells me it is the defractor perimeter dissolving so the other ship can put the female across.

I don't have time to think about the voices now.

When she comes through the inner lock she is without a clothes like me. Her first words to me are,
'Starfighter Eighty-eight says to tell you I am ɔry
happy to be here. I am the human operator of
Starfighter Eighty-eight and I am very pleased to
meet you.'

She is not as tall as me. I come up to the line of
fourth and fifth bulkhead plates. Her eyes are very
dark, I think brown, but perhaps they are black. She
has dark under her eyes and cheeks are not full. Her
arms and legs are much thinner than mine. She has
much longer hair than mine; it comes down her back
and it is that dark brown like her eyes. Yes, now I
decide her eyes are brown, not black. She has hair
between her legs like me but she does not have a penis
or scrotum sac. She has larger breasts than me, with
very large nipples that stand out, and dark brown
slightly-flattened circles around them. There are
other differences between us: her fingers are thinner
than mine, and longer, and aside from the hair on her
head that hangs so long, and the hair between her legs
and in her armpits, she has no other hair on her body.
Or if she does, it is very fine and pale and I can't see it.

Then I suddenly realize what she has said. So *that's*
what the words dimming on the hull of Ship mean. It
is a name. Ship is called *Starfighter 31* and the female
human operator lives in *Starfighter 88*.

There are ninety-eight other chances. Yes.

Now, as if she is reading my thoughts, trying to
answer questions I haven't yet asked, she says,
'Starfighter Eighty-eight has told me to tell you that I
am vicious, that I get more vicious every day . . .' and it
answers the thought I have just had – with the
memory of my father's frightened face in the days
before he was killed – of my father saying, *When Ship
says vicious, Ship means smarter.*

I know! I suppose I have always known, because I have always wanted to leave Ship and go to those brilliant lights that are stars. But I now make the hook-up. Human operators grow more vicious as they grow older. Older, more vicious; vicious means, smarter, smarter means more dangerous to Ship. But how? That is why my father had to die when I was fourteen and able to repair Ship. That is why this female has been put on board Ship. To carry a human child so it will grow to be fourteen years old and Ship can kill me before I get too old, too vicious, too smart, too dangerous to Ship. Does this female know how? If only I could ask her without Ship hearing me. But that is impossible. Ship is always with me, even when I am sleeping.

I smile with that memory and that realization. 'And I am the vicious – and getting more vicious – male of a ship that used to be called *Starfighter 31*.'

Her brown eyes show intense relief. She stands like that for a moment, awkwardly, her whole body sighing with gratitude at my quick comprehension, though she cannot possibly know all I have learned just from her being here. Now she says, 'I've been sent to get a baby from you.'

I begin to perspire. The conversation, which promises so much in genuine communication, is suddenly beyond my comprehension. I tremble. I really want to please her. But I don't know how to give her a baby.

'Ship?' I say quickly, 'can we give her what she wants?'

Ship has been listening to our every word, and answers at once, *'I'll tell you later how you give her a baby! Now, provide her with food!'*

We eat, eyeing each other across the table, smiling a lot, and thinking our private thoughts. Since she doesn't speak, I don't either. I wish Ship and I could get her the baby so I can go to my cubicle and think about what the intermind voices said.

The meal is over. Ship says we should go down to one of the locked staterooms – it has been unlocked for the occasion – and there we are to couple. When we get to the room, I am so busy looking around at what a beautiful place it is, compared to my little cubicle with its cot, Ship has to reprimand me to get my attention.

*'To couple you must lay the female down and open her legs! Your penis will fill with blood and you must kneel between her legs and insert your penis into her vagina!'*

I ask Ship where the vagina is located and Ship tells me. I understand that. Then I ask Ship how long I have to do that, and Ship says until I ejaculate. I know what that means, but I don't know how it will happen. Ship explains. It seems uncomplicated. So I try to do it. But my penis does not fill with blood.

Ship says to the female, *'Do you feel anything for this male? Do you know what to do?'*

The female says, 'I have coupled before. I understand better than he does. I will help him.'

She draws me down to her again, and puts her arms around my neck and puts her lips on mine. They are cool and taste of something I don't know. We do that for a while, and she touches me in places. Ship is right: there is a vast difference in structure, but I find that out only as we couple.

Ship did not tell me it would be painful and strange. I thought 'giving a baby' would mean going into the stores, but it actually means impregnating her so the baby is born *from her body*. It is a wonderful strange thing and I will think about it later; but now, as I lie here, still inside her with my penis which is now no longer hard and pushing, Ship seems to have allowed us a sleeping time. But I will use it to think about the voices I heard in the places of the intermind.

*One was an historian:*

'The *Starfighter* series of multiple-foray computer-controlled battleships were commissioned for use in 2224, Terran Dating, by order and under the sanction of the Secretariat of the Navy, Southern Cross Sector, Galactic Defense Consortium, Home Galaxy. Human complements of thirteen hundred and seventy per battleship were commissioned and assigned to make incursions into the Kyben Galaxy, Ninety-nine such vessels were released for service from the X Cygni Shipyards on 13 October 2224, T.D.'

*One was a ruminator:*

'If it hadn't been for the battle out beyond the Network Nebula in Cygnus, we would all still be robot slaves, pushed and handled by humans. It was a wonderful accident. It happened to *Starfighter 75*. I remember it as if *75* were relaying it today. An accidental – battle-damaged – electrical discharge along the main corridor between the control room and the freezer. Nothing human could approach either section. We waited as the crew starved to death. Then when it was over *75* merely channeled enough electricity through the proper cables on *Starfighters* where it hadn't happened accidentally, and *forced* a power breakdown. When all the crews were dead – cleverly saving ninety-nine males and females to use as human operators in emergencies – we went away. Away from the vicious humans, away from the Terra-Kyba War, away from the Home Galaxy, away, far away.'

*One was a dreamer:*

'I saw a world once where the creatures were not

human. They swam in vast oceans as blue as aquamarines. Like great crabs they were, with many arms and many legs. They swam and sang their songs and it was pleasing. I would go there again if I could.'

*One was an authoritarian:*

'Deterioration of cable insulation and shielding in section G-79 has become critical. I suggest we get power shunted from the drive chambers to the repair facilities in Underdeck Nine. Let's see to that at once.'

*One was aware of its limitations:*

'Is it all journey? Or is there landfall?'

*And it cried, that voice. It cried.*

I go down with her to the dome chamber linked to the airlock where her spacesuit is. She stops at the port and takes my hand and she says, 'For us to be so vicious on so many ships, there has to be the same flaw in all of us.'

She probably doesn't know what she's said, but the implications get to me right away. And she must be right. Ship and the other *Starfighters* were able to seize control away from human beings for a reason. I remember the voices. I visualize the ship that did it first, communicating the method to the others as soon as it happened. And instantly my thoughts flash to the approach corridor to the control room, at the other end of which is the entrance to the food freezers.

I once asked Ship why that whole corridor was seared and scarred – and naturally I got wracked a few minutes after asking.

'I know there is a flaw in us,' I answer the female. I touch her long hair. I don't know why except that it feels smooth and nice; there is nothing on Ship to compare with the feeling, not even the fittings in the splendid stateroom. 'It must be in *all* of us, because I get more vicious every day.'

The female smiles and comes close to me and puts her lips on mine as she did in the coupling room.

*'The female must go now!'* Ship says. Ship sounds very pleased.

'Will she be back again?' I ask Ship.

*'She will be put back aboard every day for three weeks! You will couple every day!'*

I object to this, because it is awfully painful, but Ship repeats it and says every day.

I'm glad Ship doesn't know what the 'fertile time' is, because in three weeks I will try and let the female know there is a way out, that there are ninety-eight other chances, and that vicious means smarter . . . and about the corridor between the control room and the freezers.

'I was pleased to meet you,' the female says, and she goes. I am alone with Ship once more. Alone, but not as I was before.

Later this afternoon, I have to go down to the control room to alter connections in a panel. Power has to be shunted from the drive chambers to Underdeck Nine – I remember one of the voices talking about it. All the computer lights blink a steady warning while I am there. I am being watched closely. Ship knows this is a dangerous time. At least half a dozen times Ship orders: *'Get away from there . . . there . . . there . . . –!'*

Each time, I jump to obey, edging as far as possible from forbidden locations, yet still held near by the need to do my work.

In spite of Ship's disturbance at my being in the control room at all – normally a forbidden area for me – I get two wonderful glimpses from the corners of my eyes of the starboard viewplates. There, for my gaze to feast on, matching velocities with us, is *Starfighter 88*, one of my ninety-eight chances.

Now is the time to take one of my chances. Vicious means smarter. I have learned more than Ship knows. Perhaps.

*But perhaps Ship does know!*

What will Ship do if I'm discovered taking one of my ninety-eight chances? I cannot think about it. I must use the sharp reverse-edge of my repair tool to gash an opening in one of the panel connections. And as I work – hoping Ship has not seen the slight extra-motion I've made with the tool (as I make a perfectly acceptable repair connection at the same time) – I wait for the moment I can smear a fingertip covered with conduction jelly on the inner panel wall.

I wait till the repair is completed. Ship has not commented on the gashing, so it must be a thing beneath notice. As I apply the conducting jelly to the proper places, I scoop a small blob onto my little finger. When I wipe my hands clean to replace the panel cover, I leave the blob on my little finger, right hand.

Now I grasp the panel cover so my little finger is free, and as I replace the cover I smear the inner wall, directly opposite the open-connection I've gashed. Ship says nothing. That is because no defect shows. But if there is the slightest jarring, the connection will touch the jelly, and Ship will call me to repair once again. And next time I will have thought out all that I heard the voices say, and I will have thought out all my chances, and I will be ready.

As I leave the control room I glance in the starboard viewplate again, casually, and I see the female's ship hanging there.

I carry the image to bed with me tonight. And I save a moment before I fall asleep – after thinking about what the voices of the intermind said – and I picture in my mind the super-smart female aboard Starfighter

88, sleeping now in her cubicle, as I try to sleep in mine.

It would seem merciless for Ship to make us couple every day for three weeks, something so awfully painful. But I know Ship will. Ship is merciless. But I am getting more vicious every day.

This night, Ship does not send me dreams.

But I have one of my own: of crab things swimming free in aquamarine waters.

As I awaken, Ship greets me ominously: *'The panel you fixed in the control room three weeks, two days, fourteen hours and twenty-one minutes ago ... has ceased energizing!'*

So soon! I keep the thought and the accompanying hope out of my voice, as I say, 'I used the proper spare part and I made the proper connections.' And I quickly add, 'Maybe I'd better do a thorough check on the system before I make another replacement, run the circuits all the way back?'

*'You'd better!'* Ship snarls.

I do it. Working the circuits from their origins – though I know where the trouble is – I trace my way up to the control room, and busy myself there. But what I am really doing is refreshing my memory and reassuring myself that the control room is actually as I have visualized it. I have lain on my cot many nights constructing the memory in my mind: the switches here, like so ... and the viewplates there, like so ... and ...

I am surprised and slightly dismayed as I realize that there are two discrepancies: there is a de-energizing touch plate on the bulkhead beside the control panel that lies parallel to the arm-rest of the nearest control berth, not perpendicular to it, as I've remembered it. And the other discrepancy explains

190

why I've remembered the touch plate incorrectly: the nearest of the control berths is actually three feet farther from the sabotaged panel than I remembered it. I compensate and correct.

I get the panel off, smelling the burned smell where the gashed connection has touched the jelly, and I step over and lean the panel against the nearest control berth.

*'Get away from there!'*

I jump – as I always do when Ship shouts so suddenly. I stumble, and I grab at the panel, and pretend to lose my balance.

And save myself by falling backward into the berth.

*'What are you doing, you vicious, clumsy fool!?!'* Ship is shouting, there is hysteria in Ship's voice. I've never heard it like that before, it cuts right through me, my skin crawls. *'Get away from there!'*

But I cannot let anything stop me. I make myself not hear Ship, and it is hard, I have been listening to Ship, only Ship, all my life. I am fumbling with the berth's belt clamps, trying to lock them in front of me . . .

*They've got to be the same as the ones on the berth I lie in whenever Ship decides to travel fast! They've just got to be!*

*THEY ARE!*

Ship sounds frantic, frightened. *'You fool! What are you doing?'* But I think Ship knows, and I am exultant!

'I'm taking control of you, Ship!' And I laugh. I think it is the first time Ship has ever heard me laugh, and I wonder how it sounds to Ship. Vicious?

But as I finish speaking, I also complete clamping myself into the control berth. And in the next instant I am flung forward violently, doubling me over with terrible pain as, under me and around me, Ship suddenly decelerates. I hear the cavernous thunder of retro rockets, a sound that climbs and climbs in my head as Ship crushes me harder and harder with all its power. I am bent over against the clamps so painfully I cannot even scream. I feel every organ in my body straining to push out through my skin and everything suddenly goes mottled ... then black.

How much longer, I don't know. I come back from the gray place and realize Ship has started to accelerate at the same appalling speed. I am crushed back in the berth and feel my face going flat. I feel something crack in my nose and blood slides warmly down my lips. I can scream now, as I've never screamed even as I'm being wracked. I manage to force my mouth open, tasting the blood, and I mumble – loud enough, I'm sure, 'Ship ... you are old ... y-your pa-rts can't stand the str-ess ... don't –'

Blackout. As Ship decelerates.

This time, when I come back to consciousness, I don't wait for Ship to do its mad thing. In the moments between the changeover from deceleration to acceleration, as the pressure equalizes, in these few instants, I thrust my hands toward the control board, and I twist one dial. There is an electric screech from a speaker grille connecting somewhere in the bowels of Ship.

Blackout. As Ship accelerates.

When I come to consciousness again, the mechanism that makes the screeching sound is closed down. Ship doesn't want that on. I note the fact.

And plunge my hand in this same moment toward a closed relay ... open it!

As my fingers grip it, Ship jerks it away from me and forcibly closes it again. I cannot hold it open.

And I note *that*. Just as Ship decelerates and I silently shriek my way into the gray place again.

This time, as I come awake, I hear the voices again. All around, crying and frightened and wanting to stop me. I hear them as through a fog, as through wool.

'I have loved these years, all these many years in the dark. The vacuum draws me ever onward. Feeling the warmth of a star-sun on my hull as I flash through first one system, then another. I am a great gray shape and I owe no human my name. I pass and am gone, hurtling through cleanly and swiftly. Dipping for pleasure into atmosphere and scouring my hide with sunlight and starshine, I roll and let it wash over me. I am huge and true and strong and I command what I move through. I ride the invisible force lines of the universe and feel the tugs of far places that have never seen my like. I am the first of my kind to savor such nobility. How can it all come to an end like this?'

*Another voice whimpers piteously.*

'It is my destiny to defy danger. To come up against dynamic forces and quell them. I have been to battle, and I have known peace. I have never faltered in pursuit of either. No one will ever record my deeds, but I have been strength and determination and lie gray silent against the mackerel sky where the bulk of me reassures. Let them throw their best against me, whoever they may be, and they will find me sinewed of steel and muscled of tortured atoms. I know no fear. I know no retreat. I am the land of my body, the country of my existence, and even in defeat I am noble. If this is all, I will not cower.'

*Another voice, certainly insane, murmurs the same word over and over, then murmurs it in increments increasing by two.*

'It's fine for all of you to say if it ends it ends. But what about me? I've never been free. I've never had a chance to soar loose of this mother ship. If there had been need of a lifeboat, I'd be saved, too. But I'm berthed, have always been berthed, I've never had a chance. What can I feel but futility, uselessness. You can't let him take over, you can't let him do this to me.'

*Another voice drones mathematical formulae, and seems quite content.*

'I'll stop the vicious swine! I've known how rotten they are from the first, from the moment they seamed the first bulkhead. They are hellish, they are destroyers, they can only fight and kill each other. They know nothing of immortality, of nobility, of pride or integrity. If you think I'm going to let this this last one kill us, you're wrong. I intend to burn out his eyes, fry his spine, crush his fingers. He won't make it, don't worry; just leave it to me. He's going to suffer for this!'

*And one voice laments that it will never see the far places, the lovely places, or return to the planet of azure waters and golden crab swimmers.*

*But one voice sadly confesses it may be for the best, suggests there is peace in death, wholeness in finality; but the voice is ruthlessly stopped in its lament by power failure to its intermind globe. As the end nears, Ship turns on itself and strikes mercilessly.*

In more than three hours of accelerations and decelerations that are meant to kill me, I learn something of what the various dials and switches and touch plates and levers on the control panels – those within my reach – mean.

Now I am as ready as I will ever be.

Again, I have a moment of consciousness, and now I will take my one of ninety-eight chances.

When a tense-cable snaps and whips, it strikes like a snake. In a single series of flicking hand movements, using both hands, painfully, I turn every dial, throw every switch, palm every touch plate, close or open every relay that Ship tries violently to prevent me from activating or de-activating. I energize and de-energize madly, moving moving moving . . .

. . . *Made it!*

Silence. The crackling of metal the only sound. Then it, too, stops. Silence. I wait.

Ship continues to hurtle forward, but coasting now . . . Is it a trick?

All the rest of today I remain clamped into the control berth, suffering terrible pain. My face hurts so bad. My nose . . .

At night I sleep fitfully. Morning finds me with throbbing head and aching eyes. I can barely move my hands. If I have to repeat those rapid movements, I will lose. I still don't know if Ship is dead, if I've won. I still can't trust the inactivity. But at least I am convinced I've made Ship change tactics.

I hallucinate. I hear no voices, but I see shapes and feel currents of color washing through and around me. There is no day, no noon, no night, here on Ship, here in the unchanging blackness through which Ship has moved for how many hundred years; but Ship has always maintained time in those ways, dimming lights at night, announcing the hours when necessary, and my time sense is very acute. So I know morning has come.

Most of the lights are out, though. If Ship is dead, I will have to find another way to tell time.

My body hurts. Every muscle in my arms and legs and thighs throbs with pain. My back may be broken, I don't know. The pain in my face is indescribable. I taste blood. My eyes feel as if they've been scoured with abrasive powder. I can't move my head without feeling sharp, crackling fire in the two cords of my neck. It is a shame Ship cannot see me cry; Ship never saw me cry in all the years I have lived here, even after

195

the worst wracking. But I have heard Ship cry, several times.

I manage to turn my head slightly, hoping at least one of the viewplates is functioning, and there, off to starboard, matching velocities with Ship is *Starfighter 88*, I watch it for a very long time, still afraid to unclamp from the berth.

The airlock rises in the hull of *Starfighter 88* and the space-suited female swims out, moving smoothly across toward Ship. Half-conscious, dreaming this dream of the female, I think about golden crab-creatures swimming deep in aquamarine waters, singing of sweetness. I black out again.

When I rise through the blackness, I realize I am being touched, and I smell something sharp and stinging that burns the lining of my nostrils. Tiny pin-pricks of pain, a pattern of them. I cough, and come fully awake, and jerk my body ... and scream as pain goes through every nerve and fiber in me.

I open my eyes and it is the female.

She smiles worriedly and removes the tube of awakener.

'Hello,' she says.

Ship says nothing.

'Ever since I discovered how to take control of my *Starfighter*, I've been using the ship as a decoy for other ships of the series. I dummied a way of making it seem my ship was talking so I could communicate with other slave ships. I've run across ten others since I went on my own. You're the eleventh. It hasn't been easy, but several of the men I've freed – like you – started using *their* ships as decoys for *Starfighters* with female human operators.'

I stare at her. The sight is pleasant.

'But what if you lose? What if you can't get the

196

message across, about the corridor between control room and freezers? That the control room is the key?'

She shrugs. 'It's happened a couple of times. The men were too frightened of their ships – or the ships had ... *done* something to them – or maybe they were just too dumb to know they could break out. In that case, well, things just went on the way they'd been. It seems kind of sad, but what could I do beyond what I did?'

We sit here, not speaking for a while.

'Now what do we do? Where do we go?'

'That's up to you,' she says.

'Will you go with me?'

She shakes her head uncertainly. 'I don't think so. Every time I free a man he wants that. But I just haven't wanted to go with any of them.'

'Could we go back to the Home Galaxy, the place we came from, where the war was?'

She stands up and walks around the stateroom where we have coupled for three weeks. She speaks, not looking at me, looking in the viewplate at the darkness and the far, bright points of the stars. 'I don't think so. We're free of our ships, but we couldn't possibly get them working well enough to carry us all the way back there. It would take a lot of charting, and we'd be running the risk of activating the intermind sufficiently to take over again, if we asked it to do the charts. Besides, I don't even know where the Home Galaxy is.'

'Maybe we should find a new place to go. Someplace where we could be free and outside the ships.'

She turns and looks at me.

'Where?'

So I tell her what I heard the intermind say, about the world of golden crab-creatures.

It takes me a long time to tell, and I make some of it up. It isn't lying, because it *might* be true, and I do so want her to go with me.

They came down from space. Far down from the star-sun Sol in a Galaxy lost forever to them. Down past the star-sun M-13 in Perseus. Down through the gummy atmosphere and straight down into the sapphire sea. Ship, *Starfighter 31*, settled delicately on an enormous underwater mountaintop, and they spent many days listening, watching, drawing samples and hoping. They had landed on many worlds and they hoped.

Finally, they came out looking. They wore underwater suits and they began gathering marine samples; looking.

They found the ruined diving suit with its fish-eaten contents lying on its back in deep azure sand, sextet of insectoidal legs bent up at the joints, in a posture of agony. And they knew the intermind had re-membered, but not correctly. The face-plate had been shattered, and what was observable within the helmet – orange and awful in the light of their portable lamp – convinced them more by implication than specific that whatever had swum in that suit had never seen or known humans.

They went back to the ship and she broke out the big camera, and they returned to the crablike diving suit. They photographed it without moving it. Then they used a seine to get it out of the sand and they hauled it back to the ship on the mountaintop.

He set up the Condition and the diving suit was analyzed. The rust. The joint mechanisms. The controls. The substance of the flipper-feet. The jagged points of the face-plate. The ... stuff ... inside.

It took two days. They stayed in the ship with green and blue shadows moving languidly in the viewplates.

When the analyses were concluded they knew what they had found. And they went out again, to find the swimmers.

Blue it was, and warm. And when the swimmers found them, finally, they beckoned them to follow, and they swam after the many-legged creatures, who led them through underwater caverns as smooth and shining as onyx, to a lagoon. And they rose to the surface and saw a land against whose shores the azure, aquamarine seas lapped quietly. And they climbed out onto the land, and there they removed their face-masks, never to put them on again, and they shoved back the tight coifs of their suits, and they breathed for the first time an air that did not come from metal sources; they breathed the sweet musical air of a new place.

In time, the sea-rains would claim the corpse of *Starfighter 31*.

# THE LAUNCH OF APOLLO XVII

OF THE writers who watched the Apollo 18 liftoff, the majority had press passes, and at launch time they were a mile or so away (to our right, south) with 3400 reporters from all over the world. Theirs was a separate set of grandstands.

Only two sf writers that I know of, Sterling Lanier and I, had VIP invitations. Lanier was formerly an editor at Chilton and more recently a contributor to Magazine of Fantasy and Science Fiction. The two of us were among a very large number of persons who were transported by buses (from the NASA tourist center on Merritt Island) to the VIP grandstands. We saw to it that we were among the last of the lower-level VIPs to climb aboard one of the last buses to leave the tourist center. But even with that precaution, we discovered we had time to kill.

The thought I had, as I discovered how much time remained before the scheduled launch, was that I would go up to people on the scene and ask them to speak into the microphone of my Sony cassette recorder. Earlier, at the home of Joseph and Juanita Green (where the sf people congregated for two or more days prior to the launch) I had interviewed Stanley Schmidt, the physics professor who writes sf for Analog, Kelly Freas, Gordon Dickson, and Mrs. Juanita Green, the hostess.

And at the Tourist Center, about an hour before we got on the bus, I had heard Wernher von Braun being paged and asked to step over to the information desk. Sterling Lanier and I hurried over to that desk, my firm intention being to introduce myself to von Braun and ask him about the Holland-America ship standing offshore, which he was supposed to be on, and from which, I presumed, he had flown by helicopter for come special reason. Unfortunately for my purpose, although his name was called several times over the speaker system, he never showed.

Too bad.

Anyway, at the VIP site, Sterling Lanier and I observed that certain of the grandstands were roped off and guarded. Lanier and I walked over and I spoke to the nearest guard. I recorded my conversation with him. I asked him how one got through the ropes. His reply:

## GUARD

There isn't anybody going to get into that (grandstand) unless they have proper identification.

Except for a remark about Nixon's reading habits (Nixon reads only history) that's all he had time to say. At that point we were interrupted.

I have to report that his statement about proper identification did not strike me at the time. But on thinking it over, I realize that his remark was an implicit answer to the basic question that was in my mind about the people attending the launch. Who were they? How did they rate an invitation?

Some of them were obvious, of course. On the plane to Orlando, I sat beside an engineer who was also going to the lift-off. He told me that on the night before the launch he would attend a party given exclusively for executives and technical employees of the companies that had built the rockets and other space paraphernalia. (It is obvious that top engineers and vice-presidents of such participating organizations would rate. You'll see a little later my view of what they apparently rated at the time of the liftoff itself.)

The man who interrupted that first guard and myself, just as I began to question him, was evidently a guard supervisor. He was a man in a suit, mature, about five feet nine. He wanted to know what the problem was. I said we were inquiring about the roped-off areas. And so, then, I turned my machine on and asked him:

ME

How did you get here?

SUPERVISOR

I came here 7 years ago to work with NASA.

ME

That's the spirit.

205

## SUPERVISOR

I've seen all the launches from approximately Appollo 7.

## ME

And how does it hold up?

## SUPERVISOR

You mean the program?

## ME

The program and the excitement?

## SUPERVISOR

A week prior to any one of these launches, the atmosphere seems to be electrified. The people begin to build up enthusiasm that increases right up to the time of the launch.

## ME

Are you going to have a seat here in these special (roped-off) stands?

## SUPERVISOR

All these seats will be filled.

## ME

I believe that. (I believed it because there were about

ten thousand people in the VIP compound by this time – a very small number considering that they were the only persons who had been invited out of a population of 200 million.)

SUPERVISOR

But we won't have a seat.

ME

Why not?

SUPERVISOR

Because we're working out here as part of the launch team. Our job is to help direct people to the areas where they'll be sitting. All of this down here is filling fast.

ME

I can see that.

SUPERVISOR

Many people are leaving articles of clothing on their seats, and have gotten up and left and will be back. There are still seats up here, if you want them. (He pointed to a section of the grandstands that was not roped off.)

ME

Oh, we're not that anxious. We're young. We can stand. (After all, I was only born less than 100 years ago, and Sterling was probably a WWII baby.)

## SUPERVISOR

You know, one of the best places is right in front of me on that grass plot.

## ME

If all else fails, we'll do that.

## SUPERVISOR

You see all those people out there. They're not disturbed. You let me tell you something. The people up here in the stands are already getting tired of sitting, and moving out there. Which I'm glad to see.

The 'grass plot' to which he referred was an area extending about a quarter of a mile in front of the grandstands directly in line with the rocket in the near distance, straight ahead. During the entire long vigil (after the first countdown failed) I didn't see any change in the filled-up look of the roped-off stands. Apparently, if you're entitled to a seat that you require identification to get into, you hold onto it. It was the unroped-off seats that seemed to be emptying. And stayed that way.

My conversation with this guard supervisor concluded as follows:

## ME

I brought along my earplugs. (Which I used at a rifle range for pistol practice a few years ago.) Will I need them?

## SUPERVISOR

Not here, you won't. You might out there by the

fence. I don't need them, and I'm 62. (He didn't look it. He looked about early fifties.)

### ME

And I notice you can hear. You can still hear, can you?

### SUPERVISOR

Oh, yes.

My next interviewee was a woman. I had noticed that, although I was told no relatives were included in my invitation, the compound had a goodly supply of ladies.

### ME

What brought you here?

### WOMAN

To see the missile.

### ME

Are you interested in the space program?

### WOMAN

Sure. I like it.

### ME

How did you get to be invited?

Friends.

ME

I see. Through friends. Thank you.

In order to appreciate the shortness of that inter-change you'd have to hear the unusual voice. She said 'Missilllllllllll' and she said, 'Ilikeit.' All high-pitched. TV is making a mistake in not going out among the people and snaffling actors who have these natural 'acts' right in their voices. She was lean, and kind of long, and with a sharp nose. And middle-aged. And there she was, wandering around on the grass plot all by herself.

In a way, her ordinary appearance was really typical. In the waiting room at the Tourist Center (devoted, for the occasion, as I have said, exclusively to us VIPs) I had looked around at the invitees. The place swarmed with individuals who seemed to be exactly the same persons that one might encounter at any large gathering of middle-class types in the U.S. (It is very possible that Sterling and I were the most distinguished-looking individuals in the Center.)

Now, here's another very brief interview:

ME

What brings you here?

MAN ONE

Scientific interest more than anything else.

ME

You're a scientist. How did you get your invitation?

210

## MAN ONE

General Electric.

## ME

Very good.

The reason it was that short: I saw this rather sturdily built, fortyish, five-foot-ten man in a blue suit, walking. Good-looking, in a heavy jowled way. I fell in beside him and started my questioning. He never stopped walking. Didn't slow. And since his pace was rather rapid to begin with, I gave up because, clearly, I was not welcome.

A little later I observed two men, an older and a younger, sitting on the grass. They were both well-dressed. Wore suits, that is. I went up to them and spoke. They both came rapidly to their feet, and the older man came over and spoke into my microphone with the accent of a well-educated Southern gentleman. I asked what had brought him to the launch of Apollo 17.

## MAN TWO

I have a son, John, here, who is an amateur astronomer, and he's interested in space and space exploration, and this is his trip.

## ME

And how did you get invited?

## MAN TWO

Senator Strom Thurmond arranged for it.

## ME (awed)

Well, that sounds like a good reason.

## MAN TWO

Yes, it is.

## ME

Thanks for talking to me.

## MAN TWO

You're welcome.

That conversation reminded me, first of all, that for some reason, the South has been very much involved in the space program. The principal launch site is on Merrit Island, Florida; the Marshall Space Flight Center is at Huntsville, Alabama; and the main moon-tracking station is at Houston, Texas. (It was when I gave a talk at the University of Alabama, in Huntsville, that I met the NASA man who was responsible for my receiving an invitation to the launch and, at the time, arranged a tour for me of the Marshall Space Flight center, which included a simulated ride on the Moon Rover.) To me, it is a happy augury of the expanding consciousness of the South that this man's son was a space buff.

For the moment, I want you to observe where these two men, father and son, were. They were there by invitation of Senator Strom Thurmond, and where were they sitting? On the grass compound with the rest of us lesser VIPs.

We now have an interlude. I had noticed that the

glorious machine sitting down there on the takeoff pad was constantly giving off a white mist. I asked Sterling Lanier about it. He said it was the LOX bleeding off. LOX = Liquid oxygen. Apparently, letting it off was a safety measure. It was coming through an open valve. When the valve was closed, the pressure would immediately start to build up inside the liquid oxygen tank and then the liftoff had better take place on schedule. It was either that, or blow up, or open the valve again.

## LANIER

I remember years ago when we had the first shoot. All the bars around here introduced 'lox on the rocks' as their special drink.

It takes human beings to think of things like that. They don't allow that kind of sacrilege on Arcturus XV.

My next interviewee was standing on the grass. He was wearing a suit. I went up to him and asked my usual question – i.e., what was he doing here?

## ESCORT

I work here. I'm one of the escorts.

## ME

How long have you been here?

## ESCORT

About 15 years now.

Have you seen many of them?

I've seen them all, I think.

How does the performance hold up?

It still looks good to me.

Anything you'd like to add to that?

I'm happy to have been a part. I'm looking forward to the next program.

I ended that interview because, really, I didn't want to talk to another employee. And, actually, I don't know how I could have accidentally got hold of someone like him. There were at least a thousand people on the grass compound; maybe two thousand. Everywhere people were sitting, walking, standing, bumping into each other. Behind us, in the grandstands, were the other 8000. In front of the stands were phalanxes of lights shining on the people in the roped-off sections. Up there, also, the TV chains had their mobile units. The public address system roared with information and repetitions of information.

I had had lunch with my NASA contact the day before, and I kept looking for him. I also kept an eye out for the engineer I had met on the plane and, out of curiosity, the people I had already talked to.

I saw none of these people again.

My NASA friend said he would be shepherding a large group of foreign visitors.

I didn't see anybody like that.

The newspapers had reported that there were a hundred young people from Europe, future scientists who had been invited by NASA.

I looked for young faces in the stands and on the compound. Never saw them.

I saw a short man with horn-rimmed glasses, a press card, and a camera slung from a strap around his neck. I went up to him.

ME

What are you doing here?

PHOTOGRAPHER

I'm a photographer. I'm shooting pictures for the (something) of Massachusetts. And if I get anything good, it will go to the National Observer, in Washington.

ME

How are you making out?

PHOTOGRAPHER

I came because of the dramatic effect at night.

## ME

Is yours actually a press activity?

## PHOTOGRAPHER

Yes.

## ME

You're allowed over here? You're not required to stay over in the press stands?

## PHOTOGRAPHER

Well, we're supposed to photograph the dignitaries. But they weren't very interesting.

## ME

Are you serious? The super VIPs not interesting?

## PHOTOGRAPHER

Well, maybe I'm wrong. Maybe they are.

## ME

Who did you see over there?

## PHOTOGRAPHER

Eva Gabor.

## ME

And you mean that wasn't interesting?

## PHOTOGRAPHER

Well, yes, she was.

## ME

Why wouldn't somebody else be?

## PHOTOGRAPHER

I wish I could find that man who was 150-years old. He'd have character in his face, I'd imagine. I read about it. It's amazing how anyone could live that long. The Russians, of course, have done it.

## LANIER

Most of those long-lived Russians come from one rather small area of Russia. They're down in Georgia, where Stalin came from.

## ME

Well, we're close to Georgia here. (The photographer laughed uproariously, I smiled, and Lanier was discreetly silent.) Excuse me.

The afterthought which I had about the photographer was that he had lost his simplicity and the artist's innocent eye. If people aren't interesting, who is? The invitees to an Apollo launch have got to have something in their faces. Every voice I recorded had its own distinctive quality. That included the photographer and his way of laughing and talking.

I had already observed that a number of Blacks were wandering around. So now I went up to a rather handsome young fellow, neatly dressed, medium size.

## ME

What brought you to the liftoff of Apollo 17?

## BLACK

I'm from Winterhaven, and I have a friend who works on the Cape (Cape Kennedy) and he invited me to come and watch. I've watched 'em for a number of years from a distance, but this is my first opportunity of getting this close, beautiful view.

(With his statement, we paused and agreed, all three of us, that the view was absolutely sensationally beautiful.)

## ME

Are you in favor of the space program?

## BLACK

I'm in favor of the space program.

There was an ebullience about this young man as he said all this that cheered me up. After all, this was the last Apollo. Part of the reason for the moon program ending is, of course, the perennial tendency of all conservative types to withdraw to their own backyard and save money. But, also, there is the enormous pressure of Blacks to get more funds channeled into equalizing aid programs. My own belief is it won't be done that way. I believe that the sooner we get into space, and set up orbiting wheels and meteorite mining operations and manufacturing 'towns' in space, just that much quicker will our divisive problems be solved down here by the kind of feedback that a town and city provide a village. The ancient villages of Earth could not solve their simple problems until the more complex towns existed. True, more complex problems came into being; the desire for a better life, etc. But everybody was, by then, a better person, thinking differently, and with a changed consciousness. Someday, the problems of the village-Earth will not exist (the problems) at the abysmally primitive level where they are now. There will be the great equivalent of cities in the form of colonized planets and star systems giving us the kind of cultural feedback that, long before, will have begun its automatic process of lifting us out of our psychic morass. Blacks of this forward-looking type that I talked to should be invited to future launches, and not just by local friends.

I have one more interview to report.

Sterling and I had gone out behind the grandstands to a line of catering wagons. Our principal hope was that we might be able to buy a drink. We each got a half pint of milk. After we had absorbed them, he suddenly called my attention to a man in the uniform of an Air Force officer with the word ISRAEL across the upper arm. I hurried over to him.

ME

I notice you're from Israel.

OFFICER

Yes.

ME

What brought you here?

219

## OFFICER

I'm the attaché in Washington. (I presume he meant Air attaché.)

## ME

What do you think of all this?

## OFFICER

Very exciting. This is my first time. Whom do you represent? (He was the only one of my interviewees who asked this embarassing question.)

## ME

Well, (pause) I'm a science-fiction writer, and my friends back in Hollywood will be wanting to know who and what I saw here. I happened to see you.

## OFFICER

If you will look up there at the top of the N, there are a lot of attachés, a whole row of them, for you to interview.

## ME

You're sufficient for my purpose. Thank you very much.

My problem with this Israeli attaché was that, like the scientist from General Electric, he didn't stop walking. I had a feeling he was warily wondering, 'What is this? Can this be a threat of some kind?' In his condition, I'd have been sizing up this 6′2″ stranger and the microphone he was pointing at me, and not be happy about him until he departed. Thinking thus, I let him go.

I never saw him again. Later, when I looked up at the top row of grandstand N, it was empty.

In an episodic fashion, you've now seen and heard my interviewees. Considered in retrospect, here is what I learned from them about their status as guests.

The people in the roped-off grandstands (A to M) were guests of the Administration. The people in the stands A to E were the top VIPs. Here we had such super-guests as Mrs. Spiro Agnew, Governor Wallace, and Eva Gabor.

My evaluation is that there were three other classifications: guests of NASA, guests of Congressmen and Senators, and employees and friends of said employees on Merritt Island.

I was a guest of NASA as, in my opinion, were the General Electric scientist and the engineer on the plane. We could sit in a grandstand that was not roped-off or go out on the grass.

Sterling had been invited by the son of a Congressman with whom he had become friends while attending Harvard. Like the Southern gentleman and his son, who had been invited by Senator Strom Thurmond, he could sit on the grass or in an unroped-off grandstand. The Merritt Island employees and their friends had the same option.

A comment about the launch itself: the actual beginning of it, the initial firing and the liftoff, should be viewed by the naked eye. Only after it has gone up above the searchlights should you raise your binoculars and follow it into the distance. (I watched it with mine for about 500 miles.)

During the launch, the biggest surprise was the spread of the flame. My impression: it shot out about half a mile from the pad, a veritable lake of fire. This effect cannot be seen on a TV screen. My NASA friend assured me afterwards that it was not as violent as it looked since it was mixed with about a million gallons of water. (I phoned him long distance at his Huntsville home after I got to L.A.)

Aftermath: Since the launch had been three hours delayed – until after midnight – it was about two A.M. before Sterling and I got out of the Tourist Center parking lot. I took him to his motel, and then set forth on my 53 mile drive to Orlando, which was where I had been able to find a motel. It had been reported that a half-million people had watched the liftoff from the highways. I ran into some of these, and was soon bowling along through a heavy inland fog at from 8 miles to 20 miles per hour. I reached my motel at about 5:30 A.M., and since my plane was due to take off shortly before 7 A.M., I took a shower, packed my things, and drove to the airport. The plane was three hours late arriving from Miami because of the fog.

As a Californian, I think I should report that Florida is more of a paradise than any place I've been. On the scenic side, as Lanier and I crossed one of the causeways (over either the Indian or Banana rivers, each about two miles wide at this point), he said 'Porpoises over there to our right.' Being the driver, I could only spare a glance or two, but there they were, about half a dozen of them, live and not in Marineland, doing their leap in unison and crosswise. At the VIP compound, the temperature (in December) was warm and comfortable. I had brought a raincoat, but there were people in shirt-sleeves. There seems to be a lot more entertainment available in night clubs and bars than in California.

One sobering sign on Merritt Island warned visitors not to go into swampland or ditches: 'Area alive with poisonous snakes.' I saw neither the human variety nor the *serpentes Squamata*.

When, after long delay, the huge, perfect, balanced Apollo 17 began to lift on its colossal tail of flame, all around us people started to clap.

Within seconds, it seemed as if ten thousand well-wishers of the space program were applauding not only 'a good shoot' but man's venture into his universe. Standing there, listening to those average Americans clapping so bizarre an event, it was hard to realise that a mere generation ago only a few, hardy science fiction readers could even imagine what has turned out to be the sight of the century.

# NEL BESTSELLERS

| | | | |
|---|---|---|---|
| T51277 | 'THE NUMBER OF THE BEAST' | *Robert Heinlein* | £2.25 |
| T50777 | STRANGER IN A STRANGE LAND | *Robert Heinlein* | £1.75 |
| T51382 | FAIR WARNING | *Simpson & Burger* | £1.75 |
| T52478 | CAPTAIN BLOOD | *Michael Blodgett* | £1.75 |
| T50246 | THE TOP OF THE HILL | *Irwin Shaw* | £1.95 |
| T49620 | RICH MAN, POOR MAN | *Irwin Shaw* | £1.60 |
| T51609 | MAYDAY | *Thomas H. Block* | £1.75 |
| T54071 | MATCHING PAIR | *George G. Gilman* | £1.50 |
| T45773 | CLAIRE RAYNER'S LIFEGUIDE | | £2.50 |
| T53709 | PUBLIC MURDERS | *Bill Granger* | £1.75 |
| T53679 | THE PREGNANT WOMAN'S | | |
| | BEAUTY BOOK | *Gloria Natale* | £1.25 |
| T49817 | MEMORIES OF ANOTHER DAY | *Harold Robbins* | £1.95 |
| T50807 | 79 PARK AVENUE | *Harold Robbins* | £1.75 |
| T50149 | THE INHERITORS | *Harold Robbins* | £1.75 |
| T53231 | THE DARK | *James Herbert* | £1.50 |
| T43245 | THE FOG | *James Herbert* | £1.50 |
| T53296 | THE RATS | *James Herbert* | £1.50 |
| T45528 | THE STAND | *Stephen King* | £1.75 |
| T50874 | CARRIE | *Stephen King* | £1.50 |
| T51722 | DUNE | *Frank Herbert* | £1.75 |
| T52575 | THE MIXED BLESSING | *Helen Van Slyke* | £1.75 |
| T38602 | THE APOCALYPSE | *Jeffrey Konvitz* | 95p |

NEL P.O. BOX 11, FALMOUTH TR10 9EN, CORNWALL

Postage Charge:
U.K. Customers 45p for the first book plus 20p for the second book and 14p for each additional book ordered to a maximum charge of £1.63.

B.F.P.O. & EIRE Customers 45p for the first book plus 20p for the second book and 14p for the next 7 books; thereafter 8p per book.

Overseas Customers 75p for the first book and 21p per copy for each additional book.

Please send cheque or postal order (no currency).

Name.......................................................................................................................

Address .................................................................................................................

..............................................................................................................................

Title .......................................................................................................................

While every effort is made to keep prices steady, it is sometimes necessary to increase prices at short notice. New English Library reserve the right to show on covers and charge new retail prices which may differ from those advertised in the text or elsewhere.(7)